# PRIME INFINITY

By

Ricky Dragoni

Copyright 2014 by Ricky Dragoni

Published by Sarah Book Publishing
(A subsidiary of Litewill Holdings, LLC)
www.sarahbookpublishing.com
2216 Camelot Plaza Circle, Harlingen, TX 78550

**ISBN: 978-1-61456-359-4**

First Edition: October 2015

Book Cover Design: Digital Print Shoppe
www.digiprintshoppe.com

Printed in the United States of America

# Table of Contents

# Rude Awakening

With a gasp I sat up. My lungs felt like they had never held such an amount of air. I sat on a bed in a small room. I did not know how I got there, where I was, or for that matter, when I was. My vision swam from sitting up too fast, but after a few breaths, everything started to come into focus. For some reason, my right hand was being held by two pale delicate hands. As I followed the hands up, the arms attached to them was an explosion of freckles and fiery red hair. She looked at me with great kindness and concern. The warmth in her eyes and the joy of my awakening showed me that I must mean something to her, something special. She smiled at me as her eyes watered.

In a sweet and gentle voiced she asked, "How do you feel baby?" Judging by her age and my apparent size, I was not her son. So I must be her...? Significant other? Husband? Boyfriend? Lover? Something in that boat.

She asked once more, but before I could reply a deep manly voice with the singsong accent of the Caribbean answered, "We must move."

"Give him a minute!" said the beautiful redhead still attached to my right hand.

"He is right, we must move." this time it was a female voice with a thick German accent.

I had to look over at this cacophony of accents coming from my left; next to a door stood the two sentries. The man was peeking out the window through outdated curtains. He stood, arms exposed, muscles rippling out of his skin. He wore a tight athletic shirt, and even under the tight garment, his muscles pushed through as if trying to burst out of the shirt. A machine gun of some sort was being wielded in his hands, and he was using the tip of it to separate the curtains from the wall as he peaked outside.

On the other side of the door looking back at me stood a goddess. She was not as tall as the Caribbean muscled man, but she stood gallantly. She had a strong jaw and intense blue eyes. Her brown hair divided into two almost impossibly long braids which hung down on each side of her head, framing her beautiful but strong face. She did not seem to have a need for sleeves either, and holding another automatic weapon were two incredibly muscled arms. Her strength and potential power exuded out of her. Across her very, very, very, *did I mention very*, ample chest were two bandoleers with what seemed like an incredibly excessive amount of grenades hanging from them. You would think she was some sort of Nordic goddess, or in her case, German goddess.

The German grenade goddess stared at me, eyes saying so much but nothing at the same time. She held my gaze, and it wasn't until the gentle redhead grabbed my face and directed my attention back to her that I could break the German grenade goddess's spell.

"Do you feel that you can move, baby?" said the redhead as she once more had my attention. I nodded in approval. "We need to move, baby" she reiterated.

From my far left came the screech of a moving and falling chair, followed by "Oi! Enough of this babying lass. We move or we die."

I turned quickly and there stood a man in full military fatigues. He had short hair, accompanied by an intense look and holding nothing but a full sized axe. He wasn't incredibly muscled, but he was made of pure fiber and strength. He seemed so strong the air just moved out from in front of him instead of having to be on the receiving end of his will. He stared past me to the redhead to reinforce his statement.

He sniffed the air, "I can smell them, not but in ten minutes, they will be here lass."

2

I sat in this small room surrounded by strangers who all seem to know me and were there to take care and protect me. It was a motel room, yes, a motel. Once it came to me, it seemed elementary. It was a motel and a rough one from the looks of it. The sweet redhead once again grabbed my face, and this time with urgency in her eyes, she asked me once more if I could move. I nodded once more also, not because I could not speak, but from the total uncertainty of what accent might come out of my mouth.

Motel, yes, this is a motel, I told myself in my head, but I was no longer in the small room sitting naked on the bed. Instead I found myself running down an alley. The muscled Caribbean man led the way running at a quick pace but constantly scanning the alley left to right as if something might jump out of the shadows. The sweet redhead was still holding my right hand and running next to me trying to keep me on pace. On my left was the grenade goddess holding her machine gun with her left muscled arm while using her right to help me move along. The British lumberjack held up the rear.

"Oi! Move it! We must get to the transport."

As I ran, I looked down at myself and thankfully I was wearing clothes. How I got dressed or running down this dark alley escaped me at the moment, but here I was. Further ahead down the alley stood the transport the British lumberjack spoke about. It was some sort of helicopter. Not the normal kind that takes people on tours, but the military ones with two propellers on each side that doubled as airplane turbines when they tilted. It was hovering waiting for us with an open side door. As we got closer, the propellers got louder and louder, but even with the ever increasing rhythmic noise coming from the aircraft, from behind us came a horrible scream that broke through noise of the engines. It was not animal, it was not human it was... something else. Once again the scream broke through the rhythm of the propellers; the scream was high pitched, yet gargled and deep. It sounded closer, and just to make this already weird day just a little weirder, I would swear it was trying to say "father," but with organs not meant to speak, only to scream. It was a horrendous sound, visceral and raw, the kind of noise monsters make in the movies, but somehow it didn't scare me. What did scare me was that is sounded somewhat familiar.

Apparently through the process of analyzing the sound, I had slowed my pace. The German grenade goddess tugged on my arm to hurry me along and screamed at me "we must get to the chopper." I picked up the speed but started to first giggle then laugh as we reached the flying machine. We boarded it through the open side door, and by now my giggles had become a full-fledged laughing attack. The German grenade goddess "helped" me sit down as she rolled her eyes and turned back to guard the doorway.

I laughed and laughed and laughed, tears were running down my face as the transport took off. I kept laughing and laughing until everything once again went dark.

# Talking to Myself

I woke up calmly this time but in a different bed. "Had it all been a dream?" I asked myself, but my alien surrounding quickly disproved that theory. I was in what appeared to be a hospital room. Hey a hospital, I know what those are! I was lying on a hospital bed, and I had once more had magically changed my clothes. I was wearing a blue hospital gown and the machines around me kept making quiet beeps letting me know I was in fact alive. I carefully sat up and nothing swam this time, I just took in the room. Well, it wasn't much of a room, more like a bed, machines and a long blue curtain. The other sides were open and seemed to extend forever in the ever-increasing darkness. The ceiling as the walls stretched into the nothingness. I seem to be in a makeshift hospital room inside an infinite warehouse. From behind the big blue curtain came hushed voices. Voices I recognized from what obviously wasn't a dream.

I carefully stood and approached the curtain. My instinct was to move it aside, but there was no reason for that. I walked to the edge of the blue curtain and carefully peaked around it. There gathered were the same faces and characters from earlier. They sat and stood inside what looked to be some sort of control center or computer center. The lights just like the "hospital room" only illuminated the functional area and gave it the feel of a room. Around the illuminated control center, they were surrounded by the infinite darkness.

The sweet redhead, the muscled Caribbean and the German grenade goddess all huddled around each other discussing something which seemed incredibly important judging by their concerned faces. The British lumberjack sat on an office chair with his legs on a table and his axe draped over his shoulder, apparently sleeping free of the concerns the others had.

I kept trying to listen into their conversation, but between the accents and the hushed voices, it was hard to discern anything while still half hiding all the way over behind the big blue curtain.

"Morning bloke," the huddled conversation stopped and the greeting echoed throughout the darkness. The still sleeping-looking British lumberjack emoted and all the other eyes turned to me in my hiding spot; of course his remained closed. My stealthy cover blown, I stepped around the big blue curtain wearing only my hospital gown and socks. Wait where did the socks come from? I kept approaching the "control center" as finally curiosity won, and I spoke to my guardians.

"Good morning everyone," really! No accent, nothing not a single hint of one, bland and generic like the people on the news.

The German grenade goddess looked at me, her eyes softening for a second as she took a step in my direction. From behind her, "Good morning, baby," said the sweet redhead and the German grenade goddess's eyes hardened as she stayed were she was.

The sweet redhead quickly approached me, hugged me and once more grabbed me by my right hand. She led me to the only other open chair in the area and urged me to sit.

I once again spoke hoping that maybe this time a cool accent would come out, but once more I was disappointed. "Can someone please explain to me what in the world is going on?"

They all exchanged glances with perplexed and concerned looks. "He should remember more by now," said the muscled Caribbean.

"We have repeated the process too many times; each time is taking longer," said the German grenade goddess.

Exasperated by their lack of answer and failure to respond to me, I stood and once more asked while raising my voice to make sure I got their attention. "What process? What are you two talking about? Someone needs to explain to me right now what is going on!"

The sweet redhead was once more holding my right hand and trying to calm me down. She must really like my right hand. "Baby, please sit down. Only you can explain it to yourself; sit and watch, baby."

Before I could ask again with various vulgar epithets, she touched one of the buttons on the monitor next to me and something started playing. I put on the headphones she handed me as quickly as the monitor came to life.

First static, then there I sat staring right back at me. Well at least I think it is me. The me inside the monitor smiled as if recognizing my puzzlement and answered my unasked question.

"Yes, I am you and you are me. Please remember this is for your ears only." Before I could ask my next question, the me inside the monitor continued.

"Shut up and listen. Just listen. Why must I be so stubborn, I swear. I recorded this for us in case they had to run the procedure on us once more." I looked back at the cast of characters around me, my mouth agape and trying to figure out if this was a joke. They all looked back at me with serious, very serious looks and the sweet redhead smiled and nodded towards the screen. I looked back at the screen and the me inside of it was grinning at me. I kind of wanted to punch myself in the face at that moment.

Once again before I could ask what procedure, the me inside the monitor interrupted and continued.

"We will get to the procedure, but first introductions. Hopefully there are still four others with you. Mister Muscles over there is Demetrious, but just call him 'D'. Trust him. He will do absolutely anything to protect you and is even stronger and faster than what his muscles already imply. Make sure one day when this is all over that you get him a nice bowl of curried goat. Where will you find the goat or the curry nowadays, don't ask me but take care of D, he has saved our skin more times that I can remember to count." I looked back at the muscled Caribbean and he gave me a friendly smile.

The me inside the monitor continued. "The other part of you security detail is Helena. Beautiful and terrifying, she is as deadly as she is stunning and for all that is sacred in this universe, stop starring at her beautiful big breasts before she pokes your eyes out with a rusty knife!" At some point during his introduction of Helena, my eyes had gone wondering and were now perched on her ample bosom and the beginning of her infinite cleavage. A grunt followed by jiggle came out of Helena which made me look up. Her disapproving eyes were glaring into mine while her right hand wielded the aforementioned rusty knife. I gave her an apologetic smile and quickly did an about face to continue watching myself.

"I told you." Said the me inside the monitor and chuckled. "Next we have Kate, no, not the lumberjack, but the sweet redhead." Hey, he called them that too, wait . . She is your caretaker, your doctor and your nurse. She will make sure you remain healthy and ready to do what we must do."

The recording continued, "Lastly we have Fox. Don't ask me for his real name, I don't think anyone knows it anymore, not even him. Ex-British Special Forces, a great tracker, crazy as a fox and with a sense of smell that belongs to a dog. He will irritate the living shit out of you, but if he says run, do as such, his nose is never wrong."

"Now that you are reacquainted with our friends, let's discuss the procedure." I perked up and somehow found myself literally sitting on the edge of my seat. "If they are having you watch this video, it means I died, well we died. Well not died, probably murdered or dismembered in some savage way." We both chuckled; apparently I have a dark sense of humor. "After your probably horrific and gory death, you were reincarbonized. Some part of your anatomy was saved, probably your butthole, and your

8

life energy saved to your totem. With those two things, you can be reincarbonated, and after three days in the oven, here you are. Now you are most probably wondering if this is real or if you are in the loony bin. You probably still have a million questions, I know I would. The team will fill you in on the rest and hopefully have the answer to most of your questions."

The me inside the monitor stood up, he was wearing all black and seemed to be in a hurry to move onto his next task after recording the video. He went out of the picture leaving me to see what was behind him. I looked back just to see the same image I was seeing in the monitor. I had sat in this chair before and recorded that message to myself. My face popped back into the screen, this time closer to the camera making my head look huge. My oversized eyes were staring back at me trying to clarify to me the seriousness of the situation. I knew that look and I knew what I was supposed to feel.

"Oh and I assure you, this is real, we are real and you MUST do whatever is necessary to set things right. I started this, you started this, we started this and we have to finish it before it finishes what is left of everyone."

After that intense, confusing and incredibly urgent explanation, the screen went black. I sat there for a second trying not only to digest what I just told myself, but what it meant. For some reason, all I could do was chuckle, "butthole." Ha!

# To the Wall

No one seemed very surprised at my laughing fit as they regrouped and continued with their previously interrupted important conversation. Once the laughter left me, the British lumberjack seemed to pull on my full attention. He still sat there, feet up on the table, his military boots impossibly clean for the great amount of running we had been doing. His eyes remained closed, well at least they looked closed. His axe lay diagonal across his torso with his hands relaxed but still holding on to it.

He sat there as unassuming as one can be, and my eyes were fixated on him like teenager seeing his first pair of naked breasts. His clothes were that weird grey camouflage that the military likes to use in cities and urban environments. I don't understand why they wear different shades of camouflage for the cities. Would a solid grey uniform not disguise the soldiers better in a city? And who comes up with these patterns? There are greens, browns, blues and greys. Then every country seems to have a variation of those. Do the countries decide what their camouflage pattern will be? Are there fashion shows that the camouflage industry puts on? Is there a spring green and a different pattern for summer green? And what good is the camouflage when you have a big round human head on top of it? Seriously camouflage in cities...

Cities... a city... that is where we were. We were in a city all of us, and I was leading us through... a warehouse, no factory. An odd factory. There seem to be all kinds of medical equipment everywhere you looked. We were setting explosives. I know how to set explosives?! Hell, who knew. Shit, that is it. At least some things are starting to come back.

"Did we blow up whatever it was we were trying to blow up?" Everyone quieted and looked back at me. Even Fox sat up and graced me with his dead blue eyes.

"What do you remember, baby?" asked Kate.

I told the hungry eyes in the room what I had just remembered and everyone did their best job of maintaining their best poker faces.

"Good, baby, that is a good start. It will all start to slowly come back to you. You will answer more questions for yourself than we can possibly answer for you."

"Oi! The clock is ticking. We must decide where we are going," said Fox moving his gaze from me over to the muscled pair. Kate had left the huddle and once more grabbed a hold of my right hand as if to comfort me. This girl might have a hand fetish.

"Why don't we stay here?" I asked, apparently naively because everyone frowned and quickly dismissed my suggestion. I guess my leadership skills were not all back yet.

"Baby, we need to keep moving. We have very few true safe places; they always seem to find us somehow." Kate looked away as she said that last bit and without looking over, I could feel the eyes in the room penetrating through my skin.

"We can't keep skipping. He is not regaining his memory fast enough to be useful right now. We will head back to the nearest wall and regroup." Everyone nodded in agreement with Helena's statement. Everyone started to move and pack things up in duffle bags and hard suitcase-looking crates. Even Kate moved, prying herself away from her favorite appendage of mine. I kept staring at Helena as she moved with a purpose until she shot a disapproving glare back at me. I caught myself grinning and smiling like the cat that had eaten the canary. Her glare snapped me out of my stare, but I could swear I saw her blush, if a woman that could bench press a midsize sedan could blush.

I sat there and watched them all move with a purpose. It was like seeing an army of leaf cutter ants clear a path through the jungle, chaotic but somehow harmonious. They kept disappearing into the darkness in the same direction with the duffle bags and cases then reappearing a while later empty handed. Well not empty handed, their weapons were always attached to each one of them somehow. After a few fast paced trips to and from the darkness, the ants had cleared the room of all the important equipment and supplies.

"Time to go, sir," came into my ear with a rhythm and song. D was standing next to me, ready to escort me through the darkness that lay beyond the lights. I smiled and nodded at the muscular figure and was actually disappointed he called me Sir instead of Mon. He handed me a pair of what looked like swimming goggles and instructed me to put them on since they would help me see better through the darkness.

I put on the goggles and followed him through the infinite warehouse. I could only see in black and white, but I could see very clearly in the darkness with the fancy goggles. How they made it to wherever we were going and back so quickly baffled me. We briskly walked for what seemed the length of three football fields or more, the floor just kept going and going. D would keep the pace and periodically look back to make sure I was keeping up. Eventually it dawned on me that unlike me, he wasn't wearing a pair of the special goggles he had provided me, yet somehow seemed able to see without any problem.

At last a small white rectangle could be made out in the distance. It grew and it grew until a few yards from us there was a doorway out into outside world. D instructed me to take off the goggles. Bright white light shone through the doorway and illuminated a path out of the darkness. As we reached the end of the never-ending warehouse, I was momentarily blinded by the brightness. D just grabbed me firmly by the arm and kept ushering me forward. The change in light didn't seem to affect him either. Apparently he can flex the muscles in his arms to move me along and the ones in his eyeballs, if there is such a thing, to not be affected by the change in light.

"We must keep moving, sir. The transport is just ahead." I had regained my vision and kept following D as he had requested. Helena was already standing by the transport. Even from far away, she was unmistakable to recognize. Behind us, Kate and Fox followed closely by.

We made the last of the distance, and surprisingly, I didn't seem winded from all the running. Good for me, I must work out. Once in the transport, Fox disappeared into the cockpit, the engines turned on and we took off. Everyone settled into what appeared to be their usual places. There was something very natural about how they got to their respective seats and settled in for some rest. I, on the other hand, felt like a kid meeting his girlfriend's dad for the first time. I didn't know where to sit, what to do with my hands and arms, what to say or what was going to happen.

I eventually found a seat next to a window. The transport wasn't laid out like a normal airplane or helicopter. There were two seats right outside the cockpit door, both of them facing towards the back of the plane. Just like in the hotel, D was to the right of the door and Helena on the left. They had settled in and for the first time since I met them, they seemed to be resting.

There were two long benches on each side wall of the transport with a myriad of seat belts along each of them. Kate had found her way to the bench on the left and turned the bench into a bed. She was a petite woman and seemed to fit perfectly in the small space. She wasn't attached to my right hand for once and seemed to be actually snoring in her "bed". A cute girl snore, but a snore none the less.

Towards the back of the cabin, there were two seats mirroring the seats where D and Helena sat and flanking another door. I carefully walked toward them, holding on to the handrails on the sealing of the transport. The seat to my right had a solid wall next to it, but the one on to my left had a small window to look out from. I made my way to the one on the left.

"Sir, yours is the one on the right." I looked back at D who was standing right behind me. I hung my head in disappointment. I wanted, no I needed to see outside, the curiosity was overwhelming.

"A quick peek, D, and then I will go to my spot."

"As you wish, sir," said the mountain of muscle and waited next to me.

I approached the window, eager to see outside, to get more information and hopefully memories so things would start to come back into focus. I could see where we had departed from. There were indentations on the dirt from where the tires once rested and what little grass was there was all flattened out in a circular pattern. I tried to trace back were we had ran from as the transport kept elevating directly up into the sky.

The transport had been in a little plot of flat land surrounded by mountains which were still gracing the side view as we kept elevating. It was the world's smallest valley and it was an impossible location. A half square mile of flat dirt with a few grass clumps and completely surrounded by mountains. Where was the warehouse we were inside of? Did I just run from inside of a mountain? The mountains kept growing as we continued our ascent. They grew while distancing themselves from us as their peaks started to form. We climbed for what seemed an excessive amount of time, and it wasn't until we reached the tips of the mountains which were now covered with snow that we began to move forward.

D was still standing next to me and ushered me to my seat with his eyes. Once I was buckled, he turned to walk away, but before he took a couple of steps, my words stopped him.

"I'm supposed to trust you. Why?"

The muscular man stopped in midstride and turned to look at

14

me. I had worried I'd upset the muscular man, but his smile quickly eased my worries. He turned and sat down on the bench facing me. He patted me on the leg, shook his head, and gave me that smile and look only good friends exchange. He began to talk and his words begun to fill the air around in me in his musical tone.

"Yes, you can trust me. We go way back, further back that anyone here." His eyes searched mine for understanding of his statement. Seeing none, he continued. "I will tell you once more, my friend, and this time I will tell you the whole story. It's about time you heard it."

Filled with anticipation, my eyes widened and my ears perked up. I could tell I was going to hear an amazing story and I could not wait.

"We met many years ago when I was a young man, but that is not where the story starts, so our encounter must wait. Like I said, it is about time you hear the whole story. I grew up in Jamaica; we were banana farmers, worked the fields with my father since I can remember, been wielding this machete here since I could barely walk." D had two blades on his back: one looked state of the art, the other, well, the other had a wooded handle that seemed to be held together with tape. It looked tired and used but menacing as well.

D continued, "Life was simple but joyous. I was an only child; my mother had almost died giving birth to me so I had stayed an only son. I worked hard in our lands and got to enjoy the joys of the sea. Things were always tenuous with land disputes and poachers of crops. My father took care of them until I was about fifteen, that was when that responsibility was passed on to me." I listen attentively, I wasn't sure where he was going with his story, but it seemed important for him to say it, so I listened.

"The first few encounters, I was able to scare them away with some posturing and waving around of my machete. Eventually things got a little more serious, and I was forced to act. Many a brave and foolish men left our lands with crimson lines decorating their bodies. My speed and precision was unmatchable. So was my kindness, I made sure they understood the risk of trying to steal our crops entailed, but I never seriously hurt anyone."

"Never, until one rainy day of April. I was walking the fields and clearing some hills for planting when a strange man appeared before me. He was not the usual poacher I had seen. He was wearing military clothing and looked angry. I did my usual scream and waving of the machete, but you would have though the man didn't speak any English. He stood there his chest moving up and down as he took deep breaths preparing to charge like a raging bull. After all my empty threats didn't work, I readied myself to scare him off with my machete work."

D's eyes closed as he told the story, and I could see his body twitching left and right as he relived what he was telling me. "The angry white man charged me without saying a word. I moved out of the way and tried to swing my machete. I missed horribly and found myself tumbling down the side of the hill I was previously clearing. The world finally stopped turning, and I checked myself, making sure I hadn't sliced myself open with the sharp blade."

"The man began to run down the hill with a dexterity and speed I had never seen before. I got to my feet as fast as I could and prepared myself. The man was almost a blur, but I reacted in time to spin, cut through the sleeve of his camouflage uniform and exposed a line of crimson red on his skin. The man didn't flinch or even check his injuries; he just readied himself for his next attacks. The dance continued until I was forced to do something I never thought I would have to do."

D's eyes broke my eager gaze and directed themselves to the lifeless metal floor of the transport. What he said next pained him greatly, and I understood why he seldom shared it. "I was starting to get tired and it didn't matter how many wounds I decorated the man with, he just kept on coming. His military camouflage was but shredded rags on his over muscular body, and blood made his pale skin red. He rushed one last time and I did what I had to."

I could hear the pain and remorse in D's voice as he told me the gristly details. "The man leapt higher than any man should, his eyes were cold as he tried to take me out once more. His speed and height evaporated as the world slowed down for me. I knew he would never stop unless I stopped him first. I ran a couple of steps and spun, bringing my machete around with all the force I had. I timed it perfectly and struck him so hard and so cleanly I could barely feel my sharp blade go through him. The bloodied man landed and his body instantly slumped down into a heap. His head on the other hand continued to roll down the hill until it was stopped by the trunk of a banana tree."

D's eyes looked at me and the yearned for absolution and forgiveness for what he had done. "I had never killed anyone and I never had wanted too, I just knew deep in my soul that if I didn't kill that man, he would have killed me. I panicked looking at the bleeding body and dismembered head. I ran back to our house and summoned my father. He made the trip back with me where I had my encounter with the man. All that was left was a few puddles of blood, but no body or head was anywhere to be found. Thankfully the blood was enough for my father to believe me."

"He kept me hidden for the next few days, fearing the authorities would come for me. No policeman or soldier ever came, who did come where some men in suits claiming to want to buy the land and seeking for us to manage it. My father could see through their lies and did the only thing we could, we fled. Father got our affairs in order, and in the cover of the night, we left for the mother of the colony, the United Kingdom. That is where fate would bring us together for the first time my friend." D smiled as he said it, but his eyes still held the pain of what he had lived.

"I remember my uncle and father having one last conversation, and he snuck us in to the airport. My mother and I sat in the backseat of the car as he smuggled us through the back gates of the airport, and he and my father spoke with each other in hushed and mumbled voices. The men weren't looking for me to bring me to justice but to recruit me. I didn't understand what they meant by it, but the words always stuck in my mind."

"We eventually made it to good ol' Britain, and we started our lives over. I went from a tropical paradise to the frosty concrete of London. We found a place and our lives settled, that was until I had to sign up for service. My father warned me to keep my head down, not stand out and get through my years. I promised him I would, but it turned out to be a promise I could not keep."

"You know we can continue this conversation later, Vincent." I shot D a dirty look, he smirked and continued with his story. "Basic training was easy enough, but once we got into combat training, my physical abilities and blade work attracted a lot of attention. I was quickly recruited for Special Forces and the training only intensified. I kept standing out, even amongst exceptional soldiers so I was summoned along with three other young soldiers for a special meeting."

As he mentioned this, my Swiss cheese mind flashed the faces of the four young soldiers standing in front of me in an off-the-radar warehouse. They had been handpicked for their outstanding marks and genetics. I was there in my fancy suit along a couple of high ranking military officials and SIS upper brass. We were there to pick two candidates for the weaponization trials of the Reincarbonation project.

My eyes widened and body tensed as the four young faces became clear in my mind. "You were so young... " D gave me kind eyes and a soft smile and continued with his story.

"As you remember, we were there to try out for the most cutting edge and elite team in the British Armed Forces. After many physical, mental and intelligence test and trials, we were

18

summoned into a meeting room. We sat across some of the most powerful people in the British military, but it was the American who spoke... "

D kept talking, but his words melted into the vivid vision of my memories. The four candidates had jumped through every hoop we could have put them through. Each showed physical abilities outside the normal range for a human. All of them were incredibly intelligent and had the right profile to endure what would be the most traumatic experience of their lives. I had my recommendation and Demetrius was on the top of every list.

As I took one last look into the four candidates' eyes, there was something in Demetrius's eyes, a kindness that prevented me from picking him to the objection of all the military head honchos. Since I was the only one who understood the process as I had developed it, their objections were quickly quenched by my technical explanations. That was the last time I saw Demetrius until the motel room, well that I could remember.

I snapped out of my memories and D was still talking. "You didn't pick me that day and saved me. The two lucky winners had to be put down after going violently mad after the procedure." His eyes searched for confirmation of his statement in mine, but I honestly could not remember. Maybe I didn't want to remember.

D continued; "I served for many years, but the bad taste of that disappointment made me choose early retirement. I was glad to be home once more and enjoying the daily cuisine of my mother. I hadn't been home for more than a couple months before all hell broke loose. Twenty years to the date of our first encounter, the Reincarbonation army overtook the world. Even though I was no longer in active duty, I was still flagged as a high risk. I was lucky enough to be paid a visit by one, one of them."

His eyes started to fill with anger and hate as he continued. "I was returning from the market with my mother and noticed the front door was open. Well more like ripped off the hinges open. I told my mother to wait in the car while I checked things out. I carefully walked in through where the door once was just to discover the house looking as it had been picked up and shaken by a giant. It was total chaos and nothing was where it was supposed to be. The couches were overturned and the coffee table laid in pieces on the living room floor."

"I knew my father had been home so my concerns over the mess quickly dissipated and went to his wellbeing. All my military training evaporated as I started to rush through the destroyed house looking for my father. He was nowhere to be found. I ran out to the yard and with three strides erased the distance to his work shed. The lights were off, but I could make out the silhouette of a body on the floor. My heart sank as the light creeping into the room made it clearer and clearer what I was looking at. My eyes closed as I hoped closing them would erase the image before me. I slowly reached over and flipped the switch for the little workshop."

"I opened my eyes and the nightmare was true. On the floor lying in a pool of blood was my father. In his hands, the machete that hangs from my back. I had seen enough dead soldiers in combat to know that my father was no more. He had cuts all over his body, his clothes hanging onto him like bloody torn rags and his neck had lumps where there shouldn't be any. His face was bruised and covered in blood, and his eyes wide open looking into the nothingness of the dirty workshops ceiling."

"The incredible pain I felt in my chest was quickly replaced by a burning anger. I could feel my body tensing and craving vengeance as I knelt over the battered body of what was my father. I gently closed his eyes and that was when his assailant first made his presence known. Standing at the doorway of the small workshop stood an imposing and muscular looking figure. He had blood on him but I could tell none of it was his own. His eyes had that dead look I have grown so familiar with that I now recognize it."

"I grabbed the machete out of my dad's still warm hands and faced his murderer. I realized I had been walked right into an ambush, but I didn't care. The rage inside of me burned so hot and furiously, I could hear the wood handle of the machete protesting at my intense grip. I took a step forward as if to protect the sanctity of my father's body, and my ambusher took a step forward as well."

"I had vision of the stranger back at the farm in the tropical mountains. I had been pushed by fear then to move fast and kill him; I was now filled with anger and rage; I was going to make the asshole standing before me pay. I rushed him swinging the machete so quickly that it could not be seen but only heard cutting through the air. He didn't react until I was close enough to strike him. He moved as fast as my machete sounded, but I wasn't swayed. He struck first, clawing my midsection with his bare sharp nails. They shredded my shirt and made precision cuts on my abdomen."

"Pain fed the anger and I started moving faster than I ever had. I first caught him on his thigh as I sliced the ligaments behind his knee, rendering it useless. He collapsed to one knee, but kept trying to attack. I took another powerful swing, and his left arm ended up lying on the workshop floor. I had cut it right in the middle of his upper arm splitting his bulging bicep in half. There was no pain or fear in his eyes, only the necessity to keep attacking. I ended his purpose with one more felt swoop of the sharp machete's blade and separated his head from his body. The body collapsed as the head rolled to a stop, dead eyes still looking at me."

"In that most painful moment of my life, I finally realized how special I truly was. I had years of training and military service but never had I functioned at such an almost super human rate. I knew they would never stop coming for me now and as my father's body was still cooling, my concern now turned to saving my mother."

"I could not leave the house as it was, it would only raise more questions with local authorities. I could also not leave my father's body like that, but sadly I could not provide a proper burial for him now. There was enough paint thinner in the workshop to at least send off my father in a blaze of glory. I opened the cans and doused everything I could on my way out of the workshop and back out through the house. I used a kitchen towel to clean of the blood of the Resoldier off the machete, lit one of my mother's candles and set the trail of paint thinner ablaze."

"I quickly walked to the car where my mother was still waiting with a very worried look on her face. I opened the door to the car as the smoke was just starting to escape the lovely house where I had grown up in. My mother's eyes kept switching back and forth between me and the house. Things could be heard popping and crackling inside the house as the first signs of the flames peaked behind the windows."

"As I sat down in the driver seat, tears were streaming down my mother's face; she glinted like the sharp edge of the machete I had thrown in the back seat. She looked at me knowing the answer, but had to ask the question. "Where is your father?" I could not answer her, still filled with rage and adrenaline. I could not even meet her broken gaze. I started the car and drove as my mother wept the loss of the love of her life."

"I drove not knowing where to go but knowing that if my mother didn't disappear, she would meet my father again sooner rather than later. I was able to use some of my old contacts and smuggle her out of the country. Only I know where she is now, and I know she is safe. Once this is all over, Vincent, once you help us wake up from the nightmare life has become, I will go back to her and we will finally be able to properly mourn the loss of the great man who was my father."

Tears were running down the face of the large muscular man. His eyes held a passion and determination that made me believe every word he said. His dread hung around his shoulders, framing his chiseled face as his hands were clenched together making the muscles on his arms tense and swell. I believed him, and in the baring of his soul to me, any doubt of trust I had towards him disappeared. I knew he would protect me, not because of me, but because I was a means for him to once more get back to his mother.

"Thank you, D." It was all I could say. When a person opens up like that to you, there are not many other things you can say but thank them. The large smile and his laid back mask once more adorned his face. He stood up and started to walk back to his seat on the other side of the fuselage. I knew I should have let him walk back and I should have just stayed quiet, but I had to ask. "D, one more thing." He turned to me, his eyes calm as a tranquil sea.

"Yes, mon?" The words sung out of his mouth as his body slowly started to relax.

"Have you ever been through the procedure, Reincarbonation?"

He bared his teeth in a big beautiful charming smile, his chest expanded with pride and his eyes were filled with confidence. "Na, I'm the original version, mon." He turned and left me there in puzzlement. The large ebony man sat in his seat, closed his eyes and tried to get some rest.

Overwhelmed by D's story and having run out of a mountain, I felt my body starting to fail me. Thoughts of motels, strange beds, hollow mountains and D's mother coursed through my brain. Along with that disturbingly grotesque and yet familiar "father" I had heard while fleeing. I looked around the cabin and everyone seemed to be asleep. My eyes kept getting heavier and heavier, blinks becoming longer and longer. First the blur found me and eventually the darkness. I fell asleep without a laugh or a smile, but with questions and a frown.

# The Feisty Penthouse

I was in an elevator, a glass one. The view of a city and its buildings appeared before me as the glass box kept elevating in the sky. The last of the antennas passed my view and I could see the whole of the city. Every rooftop lay below my gaze. The city sprawled in front of me until the grey concrete became green nature and the curvature of the Earth eventually robbed me of seeing any further. The vibrant blue of the sky didn't end and the sun shone bright in the distance. The elevator stopped and I soaked in the magnificent view for a few more seconds until the doors behind me opened.

The doors now opened, I turned and entered a small lobby. The elevator doors closed behind me so I turned, and staring right back at me on the polished metal doors of the elevator was the face I had seen before in the monitor; well sort of. In front of me was a man wearing an impeccably tailored suit. It was black with enough sheen to show off the immaculateness but not too much as to appear cheesy. Under the suit were a crisp white shirt and a red tie. On the lapel of the suit, a pin of a roaring lion made out of what appeared to be gold. And there I was; groomed beard, fit, slicked back hair, strong powerful brown eyes. My skin was sun kissed, healthy and vibrant. I was the definition of tall, dark and handsome, if I may say so myself.

Once I could pry myself away from the sexiness and style in the reflective elevator door, I turned back to the intriguing wooden door across the lobby. Beside the door was a black screen; I instinctively put my right hand on it. The screen fired up and a light scanned up and down the screen. Once the scan was complete, I heard the locking mechanism on the door unlock. There was no nob or handle so I pushed my way in. The tall dark wooden door gave incredibly easily for its size. You would think the door had been commandeered from a vampire's castle. It was incredibly large and sturdy, strong enough to hold off the hordes of angry villagers trying to get in, but also very ornate and beautiful. Carvings covered the large dark wooden door, carvings of lions, dragons and mythological animals which we haven't found fossils for yet.

Somehow with its girth and size, the door gave way to me like it was barely there. In front of me stretched a beautiful room; a grand room with expensive furniture, a glass wall spanned the whole length of the room to my left. A chandelier illuminated the room and little tables and bookshelves were filled with vases and luxurious decorations. A coat of arms decorated the wall across the room from me. It was red and black with a bridge and the same roaring lion on my lapel was guarding the bridge.

That was when the room disappeared into a blur, the light still shone from my left and the colors still danced in the background, but the only thing I could see was her. Her back was turned to me, and she stood there naked. Heavenly curves danced as my gaze went up and down her body. She was strong and fit but sensuous and feminine. Her hair was pulled over her left shoulder and in the middle of her back, black ink formed the now familiar lion. My eyes were pulled into the tattoo and it kept getting bigger and bigger as if I was approaching the beautiful naked woman, but my legs were not moving. I looked down to confirm my feet were still planted in the same spot where they were before. As suspected, the fancy shoes I was wearing hadn't moved an inch. I could see my tiny reflection looking back at me from the shoes, once I had convinced myself I hadn't moved, I looked back up in search of the naked vision ahead. Instead my eyes were greeted by a charging lion, not one made of black ink in the middle of a naked woman's back, but a real and seemingly hungry one.

The beast charged ferociously toward me and once more my feet would not move. I looked down at my once fancy shoes, and military boots now graced my feet. The hungry lion kept making short work of the distance between me and him in the grand room.

I kept fighting to try to move, but to no avail. I looked back up and no light was shining through the wall of glass to my left. Instead darkness seeped in. The beautiful morning had turned to night and the wall of glass had turned into an out-of-focus mirror. I could see myself once more, the beard now grown out and disheveled, the long hair draped across my face, disappearing behind my shoulders. The fancy suit was gone and instead black military pants and a black t-shirt was all I wore. The reflection confirmed the view in front of me and the lion kept getting closer to my shape in the reflection while my feet failed to comply to move.

I looked forward once more just in time to see the lion leap towards me for its final strike. The beast's teeth were exposed showing sharp fangs ready to make a meal out of me. Its front paw extended forward with sharp claws ready to rip me to shreds for easy consumption. The lion's mane flowed beautifully around its large head me.

That is when I woke up. Not opened my eyes and stretch good morning waking up. Instead I found myself jumping out of my seat and landing on the very hard metal floor. I was out of breath and covered in a cold sweat. I looked up and everyone was still were I left them before I went wondering inside my subconscious mind. D and Helena were sleeping, flanking their cockpit door in their respective seats and Kate was still sleeping on the bench. I struggled to slow my breath, I wasn't sure if it was from the dream or from hitting the metal floor so hard, probably from both. I composed myself and thought about going back to my seat. Instead, I choose the seat with a view.

As I settled in and looked out the forbidden window, the ground had disappeared and not even clouds were in sight. Instead of vibrancy and color, the window only showed me darkness. Either we were flying away from the sun or I had been asleep for longer than I thought. I took a few more deep breaths, staring out into the nothingness of the darkness, letting myself get sucked into the

26

rhythmic noise of the propellers hurling us through the sky.

"Are you okay?" said the sexy German voice not two feet from my face. The temporary calm I had found in the rhythm of the propellers was substituted with another jump and luge to the hard metal floor away from the voice in front me.

"Really, Helena, really!?!" I lay there for a second, feeling incredibly foolish and even more sore. I looked up and Helena stood there as strong and regal as before but looking down at me with a look of concern.

"You must sit in your spot, the window can be dangerous for you... Sir." The sir seemed painful for her to say, but she insisted I sit in "my spot." Once I was situated, she went back to her seat. As she walked away, her back muscles rippled through her tight sleeveless shirt. I could see that for some reason, the back of her bandoleers had a sheeted knife inside each of them. More importantly I got to admire her dedication to developing and maintaining her gluteus maximus, and was she ever dedicated!

# Reincar…What?

My admiration was interrupted by Kate's disapproving look. "What was that about?"

"Nothing, I was just spacing out," I boldly lied about my gawking of Helena.

"No, not that." She chuckled, "Your rude awakening was I what meant, baby."

"I don't know, a fancy suit and a lion I guess, weird dreams. I have a question and I was previously told by myself that you would answer them."

"Took you long enough. Go ahead, baby." She smiled at me and it was the sweetest smile I have ever seen. Almost too perfect, inviting and sweet but yet strong and supportive. I should have melted, but it was just too perfect and my brain could not accept it. I saved that bit of information for later and proceeded with my questions.

"What is this rein... reincarb... Oh hell, whatever you call it. What is it?"

The too perfect smile remained on her face, freckles and blue eyes finishing the expressions. Her smile finally broke as she spoke. "Reincarbonation, baby. That is what is called. It is science at its best."

She saw on my face that her answer only made for more questions, and as I started to open my mouth to ask her, she gently raised her voice and continued. "Scientifically, humans essentially break down into two main components: energy and being a carbon based organism. Energy as the laws of physics explain can't be created nor destroyed, only converted to another state. And human DNA has been decoded for almost a hundred years now." And as I nodded in agreement and understanding of what she was saying, she continued.

"When a human being dies, their life energy escapes their corporeal form. A genius scientist and his team were able to isolate the unique wavelength in which this energy travels. More importantly, they were able to capture it and reintroduce it back to another viable body of the same person. Cloning the body from the remainder cells was of course the easy part."

She stopped to apparently let me process the information she had given me since my face was making a constipated expression trying to make sense of it. I understood what she said, hell it even made sense. I just could not accept or want to believe what she was saying. It was both scary and exhilarating to think about. "So I get to live forever?"

Again she gave me that too perfect smile; there was something so wrong about it, "No, baby, you, we, no one does. There are limitations to how many times the procedure can be done and several other possible complications."

"Totems, someone mentioned totems." I blurted, "Aren't those the tall wooden things in native reservations?"

"They are, the mythology says they hold the spirits of the ancestors and the animals carved into them. At the same time, when we die, small amounts of our energy temporarily cling on to materials items we held close to us during our lives. That is why relatives always have the urge of keeping items of their deceased family members. They are literally holding on to their deceased relative's energy through that item. Eventually the energy moves on, and the items end up in storage or in boxes in the attic."

"All fascinating, but you still haven't answered me, Kate."

"Patience, baby, patience." I shot her a disapproving glare and frown, and as I was lifting my hand and opening my mouth to protest more, she once again beat me to the punch and continued. "When the procedures were first performed, they were only successful by trapping the energy at the exact moment of death.

Once the totem phenomenon was explained, the energy could be salvaged from special items for the reincarbonation. Eventually the technique was refined and people would choose a predetermined totem they could always carry with them and focus their energy on in case of their passing. This made the procedures..." She paused and her eloquence and grace was interrupted by doubt in how to proceed with her statement. After a few thoughtful seconds, she continued "... more successful and less risky."

Well it seems we have a politician or a lawyer in our hands here. Ha! "Thank you, I think. So when do my memories come back?"

"They already have started coming back, but they never seem to come back in the right order."

"How can I trust you if I can't remember you?" Her mouth begun to open, I knew what she was going to say so I beat her to her punch. "I know what I told myself, but I need to know or remember more. I think I trust all of you, well most of you. What about mister silent?"

Kate's sweet smile disappeared as her eyes averted mine looking for the right answer. She took an audible breath through her nose and puckered her lips. She met my inquisitive gaze once more; "What do you do want to know about Fox, baby?"

I answered the only way I could. "Everything," so Kate told me as much.

"I know he can be a little standoffish, but I assure you he means well." I raised my eyebrows and smiled at her choice of words so she frowned and quickly continued. "This is his life, all he has and all he has known for over two decades. I assure you, he will protect us no matter what."

"Believe it or not we are his only family; he has never spoken of anything but us and his life in the British armed forces. He enlisted young, as young as he could. What he was running away from or seeking refuge from nobody knows. I don't know if he even remembers after everything he has been through. As I said, he was young, had just turned eighteen to be exact, and was ambitious and looking for a place to belong. He found that home in the Special Forces, but it was a ruthless home in an ever changing world."

"Reincarbonation wasn't the only program looking to advance the capabilities of soldiers. As any good leader and fearless warrior, Fox volunteered for some of these programs. His body was prodded, pushed, molded and brutalized to make him a better and more advanced soldier. He gained his enhanced sense and physical abilities, but almost surrendered his sanity. Once Reincarbonation became "The" program to manufacture more advance soldiers, Fox and his team became obsolete. They were relegated to protecting bureaucrats and politicians. He went from the elite of the elite to a glorified babysitter."

I could not help to feel sympathy for Fox as Kate told me his story. But there was still something bothering me in the pit of my stomach. If Kate trusted him, I knew I should, but my memories swirled around in my head trying to remind me of something about him. It felt like a word dancing on the tip of my tongue but not allowing itself to be said.

"Fox has seen and been through all of it; all in some cases more than once. You can trust him baby, you need too, your life is in his hands and he will do whatever is needed."

# Rain and the Fireflies

Our conversation and the ten million more questions that statement raised were interrupted by the change of axis in movement of the transport. We were beginning our descent. Where ever we had been heading, we must have arrived. The calm dark night had turned in to beads of rain streaming down the small windows across the cabin. The strobe light flashing interrupted the nothingness outside.

We finished the descent and landed rather calmly, considering the conditions that were about to welcome us. D and Helena opened the side door from which we had once entered the transport, and Lord Zeus welcomed us himself. The rain was coming down in sheets and Mother Nature's fireworks lit and rumbled through the darkness. Feeling like I had filled my quota of weird and improbable, I threw myself out the door after the muscled twins without a worry of getting hit by lightning.

As I landed on the wet grass, the rain beat down on me. I looked up and embraced it, it felt, well, it felt cleansing. All the events and all the conversation that had led me to this moment had been murky, confusing and somehow felt dirty. Looking up and seeing the large raindrops through the strobe of the lightning, falling from swollen thunderous clouds was just liberating and peaceful.

The on and off lighting kept showing me glimpses of what surrounded us, we were in a clearing in between very old trees. They rose incredibly tall with trunks that didn't even seem to notice that deluge was trying to knock them over. My eyes worked their way from their tall canopies down the giant trunks to the flashlights and armed men pointing guns at us.

We were surrounded by flashlights and lasers mounted on machine guns. D and Helena's hands were up in the air and their weapons on the ground. It took me by surprise since I hadn't seen them physically separated from their weapons since I... "re-met" them. Although surrounded and their hands reaching up to the lighting, they appeared calm. After counting four red dots on my torso, I looked back toward the shiny orbs of lights directed at us and followed suit by raising my hands.

Voices kept shouting orders from behind the flashlights, but the rain, the rain kept falling on me and I truly didn't care at that moment what happened next, I was happy. The shouting men began to move; behind me everyone else in the transport had disembarked and was also acting like lightning rods with their arms in the air. Some of the men kept guard of us while others went into the plane for a few seconds and came right back out.

"Oi! I called ahead, you wankers!" broke the silence once all the commotion had calmed down.

Now closer, a singular voice broke the silence from behind the lights. "Identify yourself?"

"I told you, you wanker, I radioed in and got the all clear, I am Fox and we are here seeking refuge. We bring with us The Dragonfly, so I suggest you point those weapons somewhere else before I make you eat them, shit them and then eat them again!"

At once, all the lights and shiny red lasers were pointed down to the ground. Apologies ensued from the main voice behind the lights, and instructions shouted to escort us to the wall. The lights that were once pointed at us were now leading us through the dark old forest with numerous obedient soldiers wielding them on their fancy guns. We marched through the darkness like a squadron of fireflies dancing through the night, while the rain kept pouring down on us.

The sound of rushing water kept getting louder and louder as we worked our way through the maze of ancient trees. It wasn't the sound of the rain, but more like the sound of a waterfall or rapids. As we emerged out of the forest, there stood the wall, and when they said wall, apparently they meant it. I stopped moving to soak it all in as the others continued. In front of me stood the most amazing and grandiose monolith of a wall that I had ever seen in my life. We were on its right edge, and the wall curved and extended further than the flashlights or the lightning could illuminate. It rose impossibly high in the sky as if it were guarding heaven itself. Toward the middle and the bottom of the impossibly big wall, water angrily spewed out of it. It raged and trashed through a small corridor trying to find its way to liberty. Eventually the black and white water would find its way down to what appeared to be a small river and peace.

"Sir, we must keep moving," D interrupted my sightseeing and admiration of the great dam that towered in front of us. I smiled and nodded at him, I could not help but to smile when I heard him talk, we rejoined the fireflies on our journey. We were moving toward the dam wall to what appeared to be a man door. The little man door looked utterly ridiculous in the immensity of the dam wall. I felt like a mouse scurrying around toward my little mouse hole in the wall of a house.

We reached the door and the firefly guards flanked it and hurried us in out of the rain. We entered a hallway illuminated by fluorescent lights that extended infinitely in both directions, eventually disappearing under the curvature of the wall. I was surrounded by concrete on all sides, and my mind wondered how much water was pushing on the other side of this wall trying to get to me. It didn't matter the wall was ridiculously thick; I could swear I felt droplets of water seeping out through the wall, defying gravity and hitting me on the sides. Or maybe I was just soaked from being outside. But my money was on the gravity defying droplets.

Everyone was moving toward the inside and the guts of the wall so I followed and squished along. I was soaked through and through. My socks made that slurping sound inside my boots, my black military pants weighed probably a hundred pounds and my t-shirt clung to my body, showing me I need to hit the gym when we were done with this ridiculousness. We walked and squished until we reached a single metal door in the direction of where the water must be, along the concrete corridor.

The firefly commander stopped in front of it and reached toward a monitor and keypad. He entered a very long combination of numbers, and then placed his hand on the black screen. After a moment, a very heavy sounding mechanism made a loud noise and gave the notice that the door was unlocked. The commander grabbed the handle and panic set it.

As he started to pull on the handle to open the solid metal door, I expected an avalanche of cold dark water to rush out of the door and drown me in this concrete tomb. Amazingly the door opened and nothing happen. Why was I disappointed? Ha! Everyone started to file through the doorway, and I followed once more. As I approached, I saw that through the doorway all I could see was a wall facing me. What kind of M.C. Etcher king of place was this that you open a door onto a wall? Once again disappointed by reality, I realized it was a stairwell and everyone was taking an immediate left and heading down into the belly of the beast. A big G was painted on the impossible wall inside the stairwell.

After a lot of squishing around and asking my companions until utter annoyance if we were there yet, we started filing out of the stairwell through another metal door which had "UG55" painted on it. We spilled out onto a large room filled with tables, computers and people either playing on them or pretending to work. A small Asian man approached us with a hurried pace and a soft smile. He bowed and welcomed us, "It is an honor to meet you, Sir, and I welcome you to the wall. I am Taki and we are at your disposal."

The Japanese accent was strong and I felt that I was being welcomed into the Dojo by the Sensei. I smiled and bowed back gracefully as the small man continued. "Provide them with some dry clothing and some food, they have traveled far."

# Taki Tells

The firefly commander bowed and directed us towards the back of the control room and through another door.

Tables and chairs sprawled inside the small room. Food and pitchers full of water sat on them welcoming us to devour them. The commander pointed to two other doors and explained that if we wished to change out of our wet clothing, we could do it in private through the doors. The men's were to the right the women's to the left.

Everyone ignored his offering, found a chair and commenced to shove food into their mouths. Only Fox assumed his resting position and closed his eyes. I stood there soaked and covered in mud. I have had about enough of the squishy socks so decided to go change before feasting. I went through the door on the right as specified by the commander and entered what appeared to be some sort of locker-room. Instead of lockers, the walls held a multitude of racks filled with uniforms and clothing. Benches lined the floor space and off to the left, an opening gave a peek of showers.

I riffled through the clothing until I found something that looked like it would fit me. Of course I went with the black on black combo, but this time found a short sleeved military shirt instead of a t-shirt. I disrobed and went through the opening to take a boiling hot shower. I let the water hit me on the head as I leaned on the wall. Questions and more questions began to flurry through my head. Deduction answered some, but that only led to more questions. Curiosity turned to frustration and anger. I finished my shower, dried and put on my new gear. Black socks and dry boots to go with them. Yea, I decided to go with no underwear, but when you seem to be running for your life, who really needs underwear to soil anyways?

By now my frustration had turned hot, burning behind my brows, and the anger exuded out of me as I took fast and firm steps back towards the team. I stormed into the room slamming, the door opened and all eyes instantly went to me, except for Fox, of course, who remained in his slumber.

"What is this? What is going on? Where am I? Who are you people really? How do I still not remember? Why did you call me the Dragonfly? Who is chasing us? Why are we hiding? And more importantly, how in the world are those man's boots clean after we ran through a field of mud?!?! I pointed at Fox's perfectly clean boots as he was sitting there, feet up on another chair, axe draped across his chest, sleeping away.

Everyone stood there looking back at me, some had food hanging out of their mouths, and some just stood there quietly letting me finish my tantrum. From my right, a calm and secure voice broke the tense silence.

"I might be able to answer these and other questions for you, sir," said Taki, "but first I must insist you eat something." His hand moved with his palms open, inviting me to the table next to where he stood. "These are fresh berries from the forest, sir, our people have risked their lives to gather them, please."

The objection of the rest of my body, my stomach overruled and I approached the table Taki had invited me to. There was a bowl full of vibrant red and succulent black berries. I reached in and starting tasting and savoring them, one at a time. The bowl was very large, the size of a punch bowl, and it was filled to the brim with the red and black mix of berries. Taki served me a glass of water, as my mouth engaged in a love affair with the berries. I took a long drink of water, which almost emptied the cup our host had filled for me.

"These are delicious, Taki, but my questions". I was calmer now, maybe the berries were laced with sedative, or maybe I was just done with my tantrum.

"Of course, sir." He pointed for me to take a seat, I did as he asked and all the lights went out in the room. A single beam of light shot out from behind me, over my head and illuminated the wall in front of me. The dust particles danced in the light above me gently gliding through the air, some small as a speck of dust, others looked like they had wings and were gliding through the air.

"I preface what I am about to tell you with simple, but unmistaken fact in human history. Every great advancement in science starts as a noble and pure endeavor, eventually it mutates into vanity and greed, and finally it is weaponized driven by fear."

Deep words coming from Taki, but before I could really process and analyze them he continued.

"It all started one hundred thirty-one years ago." The white light dancing in the darkness became a picture, the picture of a colorful hospital. "A group of great scientist and doctors, tired of having to deliver horrible news to parents of young children, and after many hoops and red tape, began experimental procedures to save the lives of terminally ill children."

"Human cloning had already been accepted as a safe medical procedure, but only to the extent of replacement organs. Someone with a failing liver could have some healthy tissue extracted from their dying liver, have a liver cloned in a laboratory, have the dying organ replaced, and voila, life continued. The international accepted standards were pushed and moved to new frontiers every time a "special" case surfaced. First it was thoracic organs, then eyes, then limbs and the limits kept getting challenged as more special cases came forward."

"One of these cases came out of a children's hospital in the Midwest of the United States. A doctor and his team wanted to clone the whole child's body and reintroduce the child's life energy into the new healthy body. The boy suffered from a rare form of cancer and it had spread through all of his body. The doctor and his team were able to procure clean cell samples from various organs and were certain they could clone a full healthy and cancer free body for the child."

"They had also developed a rudimentary process to capture a dying's person life energy. This part was still mostly theory in the science community and caused a lot of stir, debate and publicity. The child had already consented to the procedure, and in interviews, he even sounded eager and excited to inhabit his new healthy body. Many legal and even political battles ensued until the child fell into a coma. At this point, even the most feverous opponents of the procedure relented and the procedure was allowed."

Photos kept flowing through the darkness and displayed on the wall, photos of the hospital, the child and the doctors. Headlines and short videos of supporters and those opposed to the procedure played on the screen, no audio played, but their expression and their agitated body language showed how much passion this procedure stirred all over the world. Newscasts from various countries played with headlines on the screen, some of which I could read, some which looked like squiggly unreadable lines. In the darkness Kate had found me, and once again was holding my right hand. This time it didn't mind, I actually embraced her touch as Taki continued to lead me through what already felt like a very heavy path in history.

"After three years of the whole world arguing over this subject and a 9 year old boy stuck in a coma in his dying bed, the procedure was done. It was not only documented for science, but also televised all over the world. The millions of cries of despair and desperation a procedure like this could quench were global in appeal and curiosity. For six long hours, the world stood as one, no countries, no religion, no nationalities, just one species looking toward its new horizon."

"The procedure was a success, by the next day the child was awake and could recognize his parent. He had asked for his favorite food, spaghetti, and was voraciously eating it in the hospital bed." Clips and photos of the child and several proud doctors played on the wall. Tears of joy were running down my face, and I hadn't noticed them until one fell from my face and hit the back of my hands which were clenched together on top of my legs with Kate's hand between them. Tears flowed uncontrollably, and I didn't quite understand why.

"The procedure, although successful, was incredibly expensive. A flood of desperate calls, letters and videos inundated the children's hospital in Iowa. The Boards pride of accomplishment over the procedure was now replaced by helplessness and grief at the innumerable amount of people they were now unable to help. Greed and vanity were of course already on their way to the rescue."

"Some of the world's richest and most powerful made the trip to the Midwest to state their fatal ailment, and why they should go through the procedure. None of them had a valid claim, but they did have deep pockets; the kind of pockets which could finance their own procedures, along with the procedure of thousands of the desperate faces and names which were still arriving by the bagful to the hospital."

"Many wrinkly faces with grey hair went into the children's hospital and came out young vigorous and ready to take on the world again. The objectors of the procedure once more started to raise as much noise as they had prior to the boy's coma. The unity and peace those six hours had brought the world quickly dissipated and new conflicts erupted over the procedure. The Board ignored the negativity and continued selling their service to higher and higher bidders. They sold it to the greedy, but justified it with the hundreds and thousands of children they were saving. The world acknowledged such acts of kindness and celebrated the children being saved, but eventually it was all brushed aside and the argument on whether this was moral or not endured."

"Over the next eleven years, the world continued to

philosophize over the ethics of the issue, lives kept being saved, and that is when the first government approached the Board. The British government approached the Board in hopes of improving the lives of veterans severely injured serving. The approach was noble so the Board listened, but now partially blinded by hubris and sense godliness, they failed to see the true and ultimate purpose."

"The program did start as advertised, helping wounded veterans to regain their old bodies. But eventually other ideas arose, how to not only bring back warriors, but how to make them better. The Board first fought it, but the money it would bring in and how many needy lives it would save was just too much to pass up. More and more governments jumped into the new arms race and super soldiers were slowly created. Selective mutations within the Human DNA were the first steps. When the limits were reached, there was the introduction of partial DNA from other species. Ways to make soldiers faster, stronger, more vicious, better vision, stealthier and even self-healing in battle."

The pictures displayed on the wall went from sad stories with inspirational endings to cold and scary. Battles waged, soldiers looking less and less human flipped through the wall, each one of them causing more sadness and fear in my heart.

"Eventually the Board had become too rich, powerful and independent. What once was a small children's hospital had become the center of a metropolis; buildings rising up into the sky with money and power constantly changing hands. Yes, many lives were saved, but as the saying goes, sir, the road to hell is paved with good intentions. And I am sorry to be the one to tell you, sir, but we are in hell now."

"The Board eventually got tired of supplying soldiers and reviving soldiers for all sides in the conflicts. Obviously, the now coined re-soldiers were not helping to solve any disputes. On August 18, 2238, the world changed. The Board activated a failsafe no one was aware of in all of the re-soldiers. Hundreds of thousands of soldiers died that day throughout the world. They were slaughtered by the re-soldiers. In an instant, every country's military was disbanded and the only power left was the Board. All war and all conflicts ceased in the world, and all that was left was the utter control and tyranny of the Board, or how they liked to call it "peace." Those few of us who escaped the slaughter and survived, eventually found each other and slowly started to form the liberating forces. We focused on rescuing people from the oppression and tyranny of the once noble Board."

Taki paused and the constant scrolling of pictures on the wall stopped. The lights came on, momentarily blinding me. I tried to speak, but my throat was dry from swallowing back tears, and my jaw hurt from apparently clenching my teeth in anger. I swallowed a few times and was finally able to get out my one and only important question.

"What does any of it have to do with me, Taki?"

"Yes, sir, I was about to get to that." The lights stayed on, but one final picture was displayed on the wall. Sitting on a hospital bed, hugging the first child saved by the reincabornation process was a young doctor. He wore the stereotypical white doctor's coat, his right arm was draped over the child and his face was engulfed by pure jubilation. The kid stretched his arms as far as he could around the doctor and squeezed him as if his life depended on it. The doctor was in his mid-twenties, sported a goatee and his eyes stared right at me even from inside the picture. I stared at the picture for what seemed an eternity, looking at every detail, the super hero blanket on the bed, the medical monitors in the background and what kind of toys rested on the night stand. I kept searching for more and more details, but eventually after much avoidance, my eyes always migrated back to the young proud and happy doctor. My stomach fell and my heart sunk, no matter how much I wanted to avoid seeing it, the doctor was unmistakably, me.

# The Berries and the Hole

I stood up without saying a word, stumbled my way back into the locker room, found a toilet and proceeded to throw up every last single berry I had eaten. The world swam on me, maybe I had food poisoning, or most probably, I just wasn't able to digest that my good intention had paved the way to this mess. I knelt there and was happy that I had found a clean stall and wasn't kneeling in pee.

Memories kept flooding back, just further corroborating all I had seen and inducing more dry heaves. A hand gently caressed my back and didn't even have to turn to know the now familiar touch. "Are you okay, baby?"

"No." Simple, to the point and the absolute truth was my answer to Kate.

"Let's take you to bed, you need rest, baby." I didn't protest, there wasn't a single bit of berry left inside of me left to throw up, and I've had as much of this day as I could handle. She guided me through the concrete hallways, and even though I was looking forward, I could not see a thing. The pictures, the videos kept flashing in my head as I walked. Eventually, she gently guided me in to a room. I snapped out of my trance and saw the room before me. It was small, a mix between a dorm room and a prison cell. I guess it must be a barrack. I spotted the one single small bed to my right walked over to it, and I think I was asleep before I even lay down.

The leaves on the trees waved back at me with a friendly furor as I lay on the picnic blanket staring up at the sky. The light and dark shade of greens quickly alternated oscillating rapidly and making me smile at the friendliness of the trees. It was a perfect day, the sky a deep blue, vivid and full of oxygen. The clouds, oh the chubby happy clouds danced and pranced through the sky, changing their shapes from hands, to dogs to a giraffe to... My commiserating with the trees and deciphering of the shape shifting clouds was abruptly interrupted by a friendly female holler.

I propped myself on an elbow and looked in the directions of the voice. My eyes followed the green vibrant grass down the small hill I was laying on, through the valley of yellow and white wild flowers and up the next hill. There standing was a very feminine silhouette with her hair gently dancing in the breeze. The sun was behind her and framed her like an angelic vision.

From the distance, she waved at me and I waved back. I still could not quite tell what she was saying since the wind was carrying her voice away from me. Whoever she was, I found myself smiling and felt the urge and need to go meet her up on her hill. I stood up and left behind the picnic blanket to keep guard of the basket and the bottle wine. It looked like a trustworthy blanket so I started making my way down my hill.

As I worked my way down, the grass turn from beautiful green to speckled with vibrant tiny white and yellow flowers. Once I had reached the valley between the two little hills, all that surrounded me were the beautiful flowers. I bent down and grabbed a special white one which had called out to me. I gently picked it and kept walking, eager to give it to the friendly lady ahead of me. I could still hear her calling out at me, but even though I was closer, the wind still prevented me from making out what she was exclaiming to me.

I started my way up her hill and her waving became more frantic, the slow full arm wave turned into two arms rapidly flailing above her head. The gentle siren's calls that had carried me this far started to turn to agitation and finally screaming. As her last bone shilling shriek echoed through the hillside, she fell. She didn't fall to the ground, but she fell into the ground, feet first, as if a trap door had opened. I bolted up the hill and quickly closed what little distance was left. Once I reached the top of the hill, I had to throw myself to the ground so I didn't meet the same fate

46

the friendly lady on the hill had suffered. I dropped to my knees and skidded toward the sinkhole which stood where the lady once had. I lowered my hands to further slow myself down and finally stopped right on the edge of the precipice.

The opening was circular and easily thirty feet in diameter. It was a perfect smooth circle carved into the hillside. Looking down into it from my hands and knees, the darkness in it seemed to start too soon and extend into oblivion. The only splash of color was the tiny little flower I had once carried for the nice lady, now gently floating down to meet her.

Sweat formed on my brow, dirt burrowed below my nails and sadness filled my heart. I felt a loss and longing for the strange woman, the kind one feels for a lost loved one. My face burned with rage and pain. A voice in the distance kept screaming "No!" The voice became louder and louder and the agony of the scream was now bordering on savage. It was only then I realized I was the one screaming and reaching my arms into the hole. I screamed and thrashed until the earth below me started to tremble. The vibration becoming stronger and more rapid, as if it the earth was going to spit the nice lady out of the hole in a big jet of water.

I backed away from the hole and prepared myself to catch the friend lady like the hero always seems to do in the movies. The vibrations had become so strong I had to steady myself and try not to fall on the ground; can't really be saving the damsel in distress if I am lying on the ground like a turtle on its back.

As I could feel on my feet something about to break the edge of the hole, my brain was sent on a ride. First a splash of green broke the edge, then more and more green almost as wide as the opening. The green monolith kept rising and growing out of the hole like a giant bean stock, this lady travels in style, I thought to myself. The giant bean stock gave way to some yellow and cream colors, a tree I guessed. Once it had extended forty or fifty feet into the sky, my brain snapped out of shock and allowed me to discern the scales.

The yellow and cream became a belly with scales larger than my hand and the body began to curve and a head to bow toward me. Two large black dead orbs stared at me intently and a forked tongue larger than two men slithered in and out of the snaked head.

The enormous snake bent and contorted in the air positioning itself to strike at me. I stood paralyzed and fascinated at what I was seeing. This snake could eat an elephant for a light snack, and for some reason, it had all its attention directed toward little ol' me. As it continued to do its hypnotic dance, it hissed at me and flashed its man-sized fangs at me. The fangs were so large I was no longer concerned with impalement being an option. I stood there frozen, awaiting my fate; there was no use running, I could never outrun a beast that size. I was the ant and the snake the kid with the magnifying glass.

As I closed my eyes and awaited my fate, I could still see the lady on the hill waving at me. I once more felt that inexplicably joy I had felt inside when I had seen her. I could still hear her voice fighting the wind, calling out at me. I could almost make out what she was hollering at me. I focused on it and made it the only thing that existed in the universe. I could almost make it out and then I did. "Baby." I opened my eyes just in time to see the beast striking at me, fangs exposed, mouth open, its forked tongue savoring me even before I was in its mouth. The mouth grew larger and larger, and as time slowed, I found myself being engulfed inside of the snaked mouth. She said, "Baby."

I awoke in the barrack's bed, sweating and fighting the air. "Baby, baby, baby, calm down; it was just a dream." Kate tried to comfort and calm me while at the same time trying to avoid getting struck by my flailing attempts to fight off the giant snake. My eyes searched everywhere in the room, desperately trying to spot the beast trying to consume me. Once no danger was in sight, I started to calm my breathing and wiped the sweat off my brow with the sleeve of my shirt.

48

Kate was now sitting next to me on the bed, one arm wrapped around my back, the other holding my left arm, probably making sure I didn't elbow her in the face -smart girl. She kept hushing me and pleading with me to calm down as she gently rubbed my back. "Baby, it was just a dream. You are safe."

"What did you call me?" I looked at her, panic was setting in again. I asked again, but this time raising my voice. "What did you call me? What did you call me, Kate?!" Eventually I lost it. "WHAT DID YOU CALL ME?!"

I stood up shaking myself off her embrace. She gave me some space and sat there bewildered at my reaction. "TELL ME, KATE!"

"I called you what I always call you, Baby. What is wrong, Baby? You are scaring me." She sat there and for the first time her expression seem real and honest to me.

I took deep breaths; well I took a few deep breaths while I paced back and forth in the little room. I was scaring the poor girl and all over a dream. I started explaining once I had collected myself a bit.

"I am sorry, Kate. It's just, it's just the lady in my dream, she called me 'Baby' and the snake ate her then it ate me."

She sat there and listened; after I said it out loud, I don't know how she didn't burst into hysterical laugher at my fantastical story. She looked at me and took a deep breath herself. "It was a dream, a nightmare. They are common during the transition of the consciousness. You were screaming in your sleep, I came in.. You probably heard me calling you baby, trying to wake you up. That is all it was, Baby."

I stood there feeling foolish and embarrassed to be acting like this over a little nightmare as a grown man. It felt very real, but it was only a dream. While feeling like a jackass, a singular question arose. It screamed at me and demanded I ask it so it could be answered. The embarrassment turned into anger. Why had it taken me this long to even consider asking? Did it matter? Why had no one told me? Why had no one used it?

I looked at Kate, my apologetic eyes turned fierce and demanding. I looked at her, into her and she knew something had clicked in my head. She fidgeted where she sat, her arms trying to straighten none existent wrinkles in her clothes, her eyes trying to look away, but my eyes held hers and the question behind my eyes forced her to keep meeting my gaze.

I looked at Kate, and in a calm but demanding voice asked, "What is my name, Kate?"

# All in a Name

Badgered and upset by my erratic behavior, a tear broke the crest of Kate's eye. She stood up from the bed and walked out of the room and instantly I felt like a total ass. I was angry and frustrated and took it out on the poor woman. Anger subsided to guilt, and I took off after her, repeatedly apologizing. She kept walking away from me down the concrete hallways doing that short step but yet quick paced angry walk only an indignant woman can do.

Eventually she picked a door and went through it, probably trying to lose my tail on her. I followed after her through the concrete doorway just to find the whole gang assembled around a table. The table was large and it was surrounded by chairs which had been moved aside and were not being used. Instead all of my companions stood around it intensely hunched over a multitude of papers. The table was covered with schematics covered in different colors of ink and maps covered the rest of the table. Helena's instruction about blowing up the laboratory and something about a code subsided the moment I walked through the door. All eyes went to me; even Fox's this time, as if I had surprised them doing something naughty.

Kate had continued her stompy fast walk away from me until she reached the security of the other side of the table and got herself as far away from me as she could get. Once there, she gave me one more dirty look and shared with the group my request. "He wants to know his name."

Everyone slowly exchanged glances and nodded and shrugged and made undecipherable head signals. Eventually after the twitching and looking party that had broken out in front of me subsided, all the eyes once more were focused on me.

"Your name is Vincent Rivera." The words and name came out of Helena's mouth clearly and concisely. No fireworks exploded and no rush of memories attacked my brain. Nothing happened; I was utterly and completely disappointed. I had expected some big revelation to come with my name, but it was just a name. Well, my name, but a name nonetheless. What do names really mean to us but something for people to call us besides buddy and dude?

"Thank you, Helena. And again, I am very sorry for my behavior, Kate. It just has been a bit much for me, and it wasn't fair for me to take it out on you." Both women shot me a glance which held a million ice daggers directed toward me. I had earned it and somehow I found their expressions cute and amusing. I redirected my attention to the maps and building schematics laid out before me on the table, as a smile escaped my face and the ice daggers became made out of steel.

"What is all of this? What are we planning?"

Helena broke out of her angry stare, "These are the plans for our next incursion."

I awaited further explanation but none came. After a few exasperating moments of silence, I finally spoke up. "You obviously have some sort of purpose for me in all of this. Can we please stop with all the cryptic secretive directives and be clear with each other?"

Helena leaned on the table, the muscles on her arms bulging and striating, her head hung for a second from her powerful neck and her braids dangled and danced next to her ample bosom. Her head hung there as she searched for some answer and all I could do was admire her muscles and breasts. Her head snapped, her eyes dug into my soul and I felt like she was launching herself across a precipice and hoping I would catch her as she said, "OKAY!"

"As Taki explained yesterday…"

"Yesterday!? How long have I been out?"

"… we are fighting in essence a super human army. We strike strategically and try to weaken it as much as possible. Our next target is one of their main laboratory factories. As you can see on the schematics, they have an intra-network link at this location which is integral to really slow down the Board. This is where you come in, sir." There were several emphatic red circles around a specific location on the building schematics she pointed to while explaining.

She refused to use my name again even though she had revealed it to me. Maybe it was military protocol or manners, but part of me felt that my name was a dirty word and they dare not use it.

"How do I fit into this?" I asked the muscled woman, disregarding her obvious disdain for hopefully only my name.

"We can handle the blowing up and sabotage of the operation. You, sir, have the capability of entering the intra-network and hopefully disabling the re-soldiers throughout the world."

"What do you mean by disabling re-soldiers?"

The muscled woman explained, "The same way there was a failsafe code to take control over their re-soldiers and away from their previous leadership, there is also a code to disable them." I kept looking at Helena urging her to continue explaining since her answer was still vague. She could see that I needed to hear the truth from the expression in my eyes, so she gave me the dirty ugly truth. "The code in essence is a self-destruct. A command programmed for them to kill themselves instead of being captured during combat. We want to use this protocol and code on a mass scale and let the re-soldiers rest at last."

I let what she had just said sink in. What she had asked me to do, what she had told me I had to do. I had to end the lives of hundreds of thousands of re-soldiers and all with a few key strokes. Would I, committing such an atrocious act, really end this? Will the countries really unite, celebrate and move on as one? Or what new evil would fill the void I was about to create?

"Oh, that is all I need to do? Simple, you guys should have told me before; just let me borrow a cell phone or a laptop. There is no need for a mission; I can take care of that from here." My sarcasm was lost on them and before Helena could jump across the table and squish my head between her two incredibly strong and muscled arms, I was saved.

Taki once more out of nowhere interjected, "Good evening, sir", he bowed. Evening? Seriously how long had I been sleeping? "We didn't get to finish our previous journey through the roads of history. I apologize for that. I can only begin to comprehend how the information I provided you must have upset you. But know this, sir, Vincent Rivera quit the Board after fifty years of service."

The moment Taki uttered those words, I felt a load come off my shoulders I didn't realize I was carrying. "One of the caveats of the Board was that when a member wishes to go through the reincarbonation process, they must step down and a suitable successor chosen. The militarization and eventual coup against the world didn't start taking place until after the 70th year of the Board running things."

A big sigh of relief escaped my lungs and I was revitalized and for once excited to hear what Taki had to say next. "Fortunately for the resistance, all security access for the Board was always biometric, completely blind and impossible to adulterate and more importantly delete. So you see, sir, you can still access the intra-network even after all these years, and you could execute the disable order for all re-soldiers and hopefully begin the end of all of this."

At first I wanted to scream yippie ka yay, run out of the room to go stop this madness and redeem my now cursed name. That is when I remembered what it meant. To stop this hell I had to kill hundreds of thousands of re-soldiers with a few strokes of a keyboard. I would have to end countless lives that had all been created thanks to the process I had created. Did these super soldiers have lives or were they only puppets? I would like to think they were just mindless puppets of the Board, but I knew better, somehow I knew that wasn't the case. What fault did they have? And what right did I have to end their existence?

The excitement from my face dissolved and a weary and helpless look oozed out it. "I know this is a lot to take in, sir, but if we don't stop this soon, millions of more lives will be lost and the billions which have already been lost would have been in vain." Helena once more looked at me, but she wasn't just looking at me, she also let me see her for the first time. The pain, the anguish in her eyes, her soul broken from what she had seen and from what she had had to do. I looked in her eyes and saw desperation and a broken woman, carrying on hoping she could change this hell before her time was finally up.

A wave of dizziness rushed through me and memories exploded in my head. I saw a Helena without the muscles without the exaggerated bosom, but even more beautiful that she was right now. She smiled, she laughed, her eyes and soul not yet broken like the woman who stood before me. I had known her before this life, she was just a joy and her biggest preoccupation was what shade of lipstick to buy. She looked beautiful and happy in her black dress gown sitting on a chair in a fancy restaurant enjoying the steak on her plate as the tuxedoed waiter poured more red wine into her glass. She smiled and her eyes beamed and her mouth carried on a conversation I could not hear, but she was looking at me.

"HELENA!" The loud uttering of her name broke me out of the trance her yes had taken me to. Fox's yelp had made her turn away from me as he gave her an intense disapproving look.

"So are you willing to help us, sir?" I smiled as the dark muscled man directed his question at me. Confused not only by the memories I have had, the strange reaction in the room and not wanting to be rude to my protectors, I moved on from the vision.

"Yes, D. I will do what I must and can to bring this to an end. "

Everyone else in the room nodded and sighed at once in relief at my response, and we continued to make plans for the mission.

# Even the Best Made Plans…

We were to leave that night by transport, dropped off several miles from the laboratory factory and hike our way there. Another team was to go with us, which they named the Alpha team, and we were to be the Omega team, poetic I know. The Alpha team would make the first approach to the designated entrance on the south side of the massive warehouse. They were to take out the re-soldier guarding the entrance, quietly unlock the entrance for us and secure the entrance until we made our exit.

Our part of the mission was to enter the building and find our way to two specific points. Fox and Helena were to find the power room and refrigeration silos and place the detonating charges at some optimal cascading exploding points. They knew what they were talking about; I just smiled and nodded. It was over my head, and they tried to explain that if they placed a few charges at the optimal points, it would create an exponentially growing domino effect which would take out the whole facility. Or how I described it back to them, "You guys make the place go boom."

Kate, D and I were to find the control center, and in there find the only computer connected to the intra-network, easy enough right. Once there, D would provide security for me as I logged on and sent out a disable code, which I had absolutely no clue what it was. Easy, I know. I protested at Kate's involvement in the mission, I hadn't seen the girl lift a gun or even show me a sliver of potential violence in her. My objections were instantly and aggressively revoked by the group, and even Kate in her own sweet way made it clear that she must be there. I didn't know what reason or purpose this girl would have in such a place, but I was clearly overruled by everyone.

Once all plans were made, I felt obligated to point out the ridiculousness and suicidal properties of the mission at hand. Once more I was met with defiant eyes and assured it would all be okay.

I didn't believe them for a second, but I had made this hell and I had to end it. If I had to die doing it, I had lived long enough. How long have I lived? I mean I was mid-twenties in the photo I saw on the slide show and that was one hundred thirty-one years ago. Holy buckets! I was one hundred fifty plus years old, that is pretty cool, too bad senility had claimed my memories. Well some of them. I felt like a vampire living through the centuries, but I also felt tired and okay if it was my time for it to end. Ha! Age can take my memories but not my wisdom.

Everyone left the room and went to gear up, whatever that meant. Since I had just been like a runway model recently in a wardrobe changing frenzy, including a hospital gown and wet socks, I decided to find my way to the cafeteria for some food and stay with my current outfit. If I was going to die, I was going to die on a full stomach. As before, the tables were covered in food. All of the food was in wrappers, cans or dehydrated, but it was food. Thankfully the bowl of berries wasn't there to mock me. I found some breakfast toaster pastries and ate them cold as they were: strawberry, my favorite. I found a few more prepackaged items, which I fancied, and indulged in what might be my last dinner. As I sat there drinking some water with a full and content belly, D walked in. "You ready, sir?"

"Nope, not one bit."

He laughed and his laugh rich and deep filled the room and made me smile. "No one is really ever ready for something like this, sir. May I call you Vincent?"

Ecstatic and with a growing smile, "Yes, please!" I replied to him.

"Well, Vincent, my friend, as I said, no one is ever truly ready for something like this, but the important part is that you have the will to carry it through and the conviction to see it to its end, no matter what that end might be. I will reassure you with this, Vincent, I will protect you and be with you whether we end up

58

back here eating more crummy food or whether we both bleed to death next to each other out there."

The big muscular man smiled and never had a more gruesome promise made anyone feel more at peace than I felt that second.

"It's time to go... Mon." He smiled as he said it and I could not help but smile from ear to ear. "You always loved it when I call you Mon, now time to get dirty, Vincent."

I stood up and followed him with a resolve and confidence I didn't know I had. I followed the mountainous man out of the room, smiling and happy, not caring what fate had in store for me because I knew I had D to protect me and make me smile. Ha! He said Mon, I love it!

Everyone loaded into the transport like before. Only this time Kate's bed was covered in well-armed men's butts. We flew in the darkness like before, but the jog over to the transport and out of the concrete juggernaut was speckled with stars instead of flying mud from boots.

I sat in "my spot" as we flew and everyone else filled in into where they belonged as well. Not a word was uttered and you could cut the tension emanating out of everyone with a knife. Helena was deep in thought, staring out her little window. Kate sat in the chair next to mine across the alleyway. She slept, whether it was her way of relaxing or she was just exhausted from the early drama, the sweet redhead was fast asleep. Across the way, D laid his head back and was half to this world. Every once in a while, he would open his eyes, fully engage me in a comforting smile and go back to his resting position. The Alpha team sat on the benches and stared straight ahead, holding their weapons looking like statues, only the swaying of the plane gave away that they were made out of flesh and bone.

We flew for an eternity, well it felt like an eternity, it was hours, well more like one hour and a little bit, but it was an eternity; that's my story and I am sticking with it. We landed on a grassy plain. As we opened the door and were able to take a peak of the outside, all of the tall grass bowed in front of the metal bird in which we had arrived. Everyone disembarked with military precision, except me of course; I was being babysat by both Kate and D. Under any other circumstances, I would have asked for some space and complained that I was an adult. But being where we were and what was about to happen, I allowed the babysitting to continue.

Everyone escaped the turbines and wind from the transport as they made their way into the woods. The transport engines came to halt, and Fox eventually disembarked the flying metal can. He waded confidently through the now waist high grass holding nothing but his axe. He met us in the woods, the plan was quickly reviewed, and we were on our way. Adrenaline was pumping and every sound and every shadow was amplified and terrifying. After thirty minutes or so of walking through the woods, the all famous adrenaline dump was kicking my ass. I was ready to get out of the transport, engage in action and save the world. Instead I spent all that gung ho energy I had going for me on a hushed walk through the freaking woods.

Fear, doubt and anxiety were now settling in just in time for us to reach the edge of the woods and getting our first glimpse at our targeted location. We stood at the top of a ridge and down in the valley was the warehouse. All the drawings and maps did not prepare me for what sprawled in front of us. We had to be a good one hundred yards away and all you could see to the left and to the right was the facility. I had expected a large building, but this needed a different adjective other than large. It occupied my field of view from left to right and it extended in front of us so far that the safety lights in the roof eventually began to blend with the night's stars.

It was a very calm and beautiful night. The stars twinkled

above, and out here with very few lights, I could even get a peak of the famous Milky Way. The night was cool but not chilly. The wind blew just barely enough to keep providing us with fresh air. It was the perfect kind of a night for a date, cool enough to snuggle, a beautiful sky and as tranquil as one could ever ask for. Instead of a romantic date or a calm nap under the stars, we were about to walk into the facility with the same chance of survival as a cow has escaping a slaughterhouse alive.

# Axe, Camera, Action!

The Alpha team exchanged some last few hushed words with Helena and started to make their way down the ridge toward the facility. They slowly flared out from each other to cover more ground in their descent down the hill until they were walking with choreographed precision while being yards away from each other.

Everyone still with me seemed to have spawned binoculars out of nowhere and were closely following the movement of team Alpha. Before I could complain and request a pair, Kate provided me with my own pair. I quickly held them up to my eyes, scanned left and right up and down until I set my sights on the building and where the Alpha team was heading. A simple man-door was all there was and a single unarmed guard at first inspection is all that was preventing us from getting into the building.

The guard, if you could call him that, stood leaning against the wall completely unassuming and without any apparent care in the world. He looked more like a loiterer than a guard, but his lack of care gave off a confidence that made it clear he was dangerous. He took a drag of a cigarette and let the smoke billow out of his mouth slowly. He should quit that awful habit; it is going to kill him. Ha! What am I talking about?! The Alpha team is going to take care of that for him. He wore blue jeans and a white t-shirt, and even though it wasn't that chilly, he had to be cold sitting out here leaning on a dead concrete wall.

The Alpha team continued their graceful approach and started to form a semi-circle heading directly towards the door. Lights started flashing from the muzzle of all the guns of the Alpha team, no sound came roaring to us, but the lights kept flashing on and off rapidly. I followed the flashes toward where the guns where pointed, and the guard that once stood by the door now jerked and flailed as he was receiving the impact of all the bullets. He kept twitching, dancing and jerking around while bullet after bullet impaled itself inside his body, yet he didn't fall. The team continued to advance, and the guard started to charge them. The flashes and the jerking continued and there was no reason this man shouldn't have been dead one hundred bullets ago, and yet he was not only standing but walking in the direction of the fire.

The two edge men of the Alpha team semicircle broke ranks and started to flank and approach the guard closer. As they reached the guard, the rest of the team's guns stopped flashing and the two soldiers rushed the guard producing edged weapons out of nowhere. One of them held a machete while the other wielded a katana sword. They moved incredibly fast and it was hard to keep track of it all through the binoculars.

When I was able to re-find the action through the binoculars, the two soldiers lay dead on the ground. I knew they were dead since the one wielding the machete was now in two pieces. His legs were behind the guard while his torso lay in front of the guard, guts and blood spilling out of it. The soldier wielding the katana had a hole the size of a cannonball through his chest and was just off to the right of the guard. The guard was now covered in blood, of which very little seemed to be his, and the flashing lights on the tips of the guns of the Alpha team started once more, like desperate meteor shower.

The team kept advancing on the guard, emptying magazine after magazine of bullets into the bulletproof guard. The next two soldiers broke rank from the semicircle's edge and advanced on the re-soldier. Once more they found their fate to be body parts and puddles of blood in the grass. The re-soldier moved faster than what my eyes could follow and stood there absorbing the impact of the endless rain of bullets.

A mumbled cursed came from my right and made me jump. I had been so mesmerized by what I was seeing on the other end of the binoculars that I had forgotten I was surrounded by my own team. Fox kept mumbling and cursing as he trotted his way down the ridge to where the re-soldier and the ever-diminishing Alpha squadron engaged on their stalemate of bullets versus inhuman speed. The only other person to have pried her eyes away from her binoculars was Kate, she gave me a smile and shrug and went back to viewing the action.

I followed Kate's lead and once more started viewing the impossible reality taking place on the other end of the binoculars. Fox picked up speed and momentum as he approached the action. His usually paperweight of an axe was now being wielded and swung around with increasing speed as he was now sprinting towards the re-soldier. He dangerously approached the curtain of bullets emanating from the flashing machineguns, the flashing stopped once they noticed him approaching. He moved almost as impossibly fast as I had seen the re-soldier move through he binoculars, he leapt while spinning in the air, did two or three revolutions in the air, it was hard to count with him moving so fast, and landed axe extended, legs squatted and his free left arm held at a 90 degree angle at the elbow for balance.

Quite dramatic and a little ridiculous if you ask me, spinning and landing like ninja with axe, just to make an entrance. Fox hadn't struck me as the kind for theatrics, but we all have our hidden quirks. That is when I noticed the re-soldier was no longer slowly advancing toward the Alpha team; instead it was just standing there gently swaying from side to side. The re-soldier swayed a couple more times as Fox stayed in his dramatic pose and then the body of the re-soldier crumpled to its right as the head gently tipped over the neck, fell to the left and rolled for a few feet.

As the head came to a rest looking like a misshaped bowling ball on the grass, Fox stood and proceeded to direct some furious, and if I were guessing, curse laden instructions at what remained of the Alpha team. Even through the binoculars, I could see them nodding and their bodies tense with fear at his instruction. Once he seemed to be done, they all moved in different directions and

64

started cleaning up the gory mess that lay at their feet.

The amazing acrobatics and quick dispatch of the re-soldier brought back a rush of memories. I had seen that move once before and behind it a pair of desperate eyes. We had started to look for volunteers for the Reincarbonation program, and he had been one of the first volunteers. Special Forces leapt at the opportunity to become more "special."

I was standing in a hangar along some uniformed men with a lot of stripes and medals on their coats. I had told them I wanted to meet the candidates but didn't expect for it to turn into a talent show. I would get a briefing on each candidate, given a file with their information, they would come out and show off their talents and then I would interview them. Most of them were at the end of their career looking for a way to extend it. They were formidable soldiers, but they had seen too much. Their minds corrupted with violence which no human should ever see. The scars and broken bones they had paled in comparison to the wounds inside their minds.

I had made it clear in meeting after meeting that we needed blank canvases as volunteers for this program. They disagreed and insisted on these candidates, and so now I sat there and watched the parade of marksmanship and weapons demonstrations. Once I was finally able to sit down with every candidate, the same pair of dead eyes stared back at me from across the table. Every question was answered with "Sir" or "Yes, Sir." It was a little disconcerting how they talked and acted more like robots than humans anymore. I know they were trying to impress me, but all they achieved was to make me sad.

I felt sad for what was left in front of me; they were not humans anymore. What they must have seen and lived to leave them this cold and closed to what they once were. With each set of dead eyes, my point was made stronger and stronger. The fancy uniformed men kept trying to focus on the skills and experience, but with every one of my questions, even they saw that we could not bring back these candidates. They were not human anymore, they were broken monsters and the Reincarbonation process would only make that worse.

I was ready to leave this parade of skill and sadness, but I was assured they had left the best for last and I had to meet this candidate. I was handed the simple looking tan folder. It looked like every other one I had been handed over the past ten hours. I opened it, and unlike the others, there was no first name and last name, just a code name "Fox." I was intrigued, so I pushed aside the frustration of the day and read the file with an open mind.

Before I could dive much into the file, a man wearing green camouflage fatigues and sporting only an axe was standing before us. He went through the rigmarole of his routine ending with a fancy flying pirouette and finishing with the decapitation of a poor dummy with his axe. It was theatric and exaggerated, but he did move with a speed I hadn't seen in any of the other candidates. Once done, he stood at attention until he was ordered over.

I recognized his face more and more with every step he took toward the table where I sat. Once he was sitting in front of me, there was no doubt in my mind of who he really was. His face had headlined many a newspaper and magazines. Numerous scandalous reports were told all over the international press. I thought the stories of his reformation had been greatly exaggerated, but yet here he sat in front of me, the perfect soldier for country and King.

I looked around the table, and every nod and look I got back confirmed I wasn't crazy. It was Prince Albert. He was sixth in line to the crown and that was before babies on the way would push him even further down the totem pole. The stories of his exuberance and shenanigans were the talk of the world really. Realizing he would never ever get to wear the crown, Prince Albert had decided to make the most of his status as royalty and a young single man. There were really few transgressions that he didn't commit, well at least didn't get caught. Every week, it seemed the tabloids and even the mainstream media were reporting on his latest escapade or who he was romantically involved with now.

Prince Albert took full advantage of his status, clout and looks to completely embarrass the crown, and so became the Royal Family black sheep. It wasn't until after the car accident that his reformation began. When it happened, you could not watch any newscast, read any print or even open an internet browser without his name and face being plastered all over it. It had been another night of drinking and partying. He was out with a very popular actress, so the paparazzi were out in full force to cover what could be his latest transgression, and he didn't disappoint.

Refusing to be driven, even though he was very intoxicated, he got behind the wheel of his Rolls Royce. He made sure to give the paparazzi some material, groping and almost undressing his latest but most famous conquest. He sped off, some of the media followed, but few could follow at the speeds at which he was driving. Eventually the trailing reporters caught up to him, as well as the police and paramedics. The expensive chariot had run into an old oak tree and had taken the full force of nature.

Prince Albert was badly hurt, but the real story was his companion. The once beautiful face, who had been projected onto movie screens thousands of times, was now just a mangled bloody mess. Her body was broken and her heart had stop beating. The media had a field day with the tragedy, and the Royal Family was shamed far beyond their wildest dreams. Prince Albert disappeared from the limelight and into private medical care. He had survived the accident, but not by much. It took months of medical care and rehabilitation before he was even capable of going before the bright lights to issue his heartfelt apology.

I remember it was on every channel, as if the president of a country had been making an important speech. Instead it was a lowly prince from an obsolete tradition who was nothing more than a stupid kid. His good looks had suffered from the crash. Not even the best plastic surgeons could hide all the scars that were left. Once the teary apology finished, the media scrutinized every word and gesture of his speech, and the masses started to campaign for his forgiveness.

The world being what it is, he never went to trial; instead in an act of contrition, he enlisted to serve his country. That was to be his punishment and penance for the murder of the poor starlet. There was a little outcry over it, but for some reason, most were satisfied and Prince Albert slowly melted into oblivion. I always felt it was bullshit, and he was truly just hiding in some chateaux still living the good life. Instead the young idiot now sat in front of me as the definition of what a soldier should be.

The interview was awkward to say the least. All of the other candidates, I had no clue who they were, but I knew Prince Albert and had to truly refrain from asking him all the impertinent questions I wanted to ask about his past. It took a lot of self-control, but I got through it. Once he was gone, all of the upper brass let me look through his file at my leisure. I had to admit the once black sheep of the Royal Family was the only viable candidate out of the bunch. Everyone was offended that he was the only one I wanted to bring into the program, but I had final say, so they had to deal with it.

So it began the slippery slope which would send the whole world into turmoil. The British military spent millions building the facility I requested, it had everything I had asked for all housed in a 30,000 square meter facility. It wasn't really a laboratory, it was really a complex. Fox showed up as requested, and it was just him, me and my assistants in the gigantic facility. He showed up the perfect formal soldier, and now it was my turn to tear him down and build him up over and over. Not only mentally, but on a molecular and genetic scale. The military wanted their Re-Soldier, as it was coined, fast, but I was going to take my time to make sure I did it right.

I ran every test, screening and procedure I could think of. This was going to be the first procedure of its kind, so I spared no expense; after all it was the government's money. I knew Fox was the perfect candidate, but I continued to come up with ways to delay the procedure. I knew the science was sound, the candidate was right and ready, but the reality of what I had to do paralyzed me.

With much pressure from the people lining my pockets and out of plausible delays, I had to face what my life had become. We did one last physical on Fox and there he lay on the cold metal examination table. I stood in that spot before, but with dying and sick patients, not with a healthy soldier who was the standard for good health. I had to kill a man just so I could bring him back a better killer, and it was tearing me apart inside. I had to keep thinking of all the lives I was saving by me killing and twisting this one.

Fox's eyes were fixated on the ceiling, lost in his thoughts and determination. His trance broke at my lingering hesitation and our eyes met. Through all of our screenings, interviews and tests, Fox the black sheep prince had been the definition of formality and military protocol. His answers were always short, precise and clear. He never asked questions nor challenged anything he was asked or ordered to do. His total obedience and loyalty to the crown was what made him the perfect candidate, even when he had the feeling of automaton.

As his intense eyes dug into my soul for the first and last time, Fox showed me some true humanity.

"It is okay, Doc."

Four simple words that said so much. My soul was heavy, but I nodded in agreement and started the procedure.

I hooked him up to the IV, prepared the chemical and rolled him into the Reincarbonation chamber. The chamber looked like a mix of a coffin and a giant gel tablet. Fox fit snugly in the futuristic escape pod while still on the examination gurney. My hands were starting to tremble as they approached the button for the first dosage. I would put Fox under general anesthesia then release the pancuronium bromide and finish with the potassium chloride. It was the same cocktail convicted murderers received as part of their death sentence, which made me feel ever more like an executioner rather than a healer.

Fox's eyes closed, and as the other chemicals were released, I expected his body to start jumping and have spasms inside the chamber. Instead his body was placid and calm, and for once, the ever present scowl on his forehead had relaxed. The only noise in the room was the rhythmic beeping of the machinery telling me he was just asleep. I jumped as the chemical dispenser made a hissing sound, beginning to pump the last and lethal chemical into Fox's body.

I could feel my heart trying to explode out of my chest as the chemical slowly made its way down the clear plastic tube and into Fox's veins. Enough time had passed, but nothing happened. I read the display to make sure potassium chloride had been released and it had. Still Fox's heartbeat at the same relaxed rate and mine beat so hard and fast I could feel it in the veins on my forehead. I shook the dispenser and kept fiddling with it when the slowly accelerating beeping made me stop dead in my tracks. I looked back at Fox and he still looked peaceful and relaxed inside the chamber.

The monitor's pace kept picking up until our accelerated heartbeats danced in unison, mine out of fear and guilt, and his out of impending death. The beeping and beating grew faster and louder, filling the room with its high frequency. His body kept fighting to survive, too foolish to know it was an impossible fight. The fast beats from the machine grew faster and faster until the beeping desisted and all but the monotone sound of death filled the air. My heart kept beating faster as my ears were assaulted by the high pitched constant sound. The room began to swim and spin on me. My vision narrowed, making me feel as if I were looking out from a tunnel.

I took a long deep breath and closed my eyes, my hands firmly holding onto the handles of the chamber where the dead man rested. I had just killed a man and my body was trying real hard to expel my soul and intellect out of it. I swallowed the bile coming up my esophagus, shook away the dizziness, and slowly calmed down my panicked heart. I had to focus so I could finish the procedure and bring Fox back.

I slowly opened my eyes and things thankfully stayed in one place. The room no longer danced in front of my eyes and the cold sweats had stopped. I prepared the chamber and began the Reincarbonation. It was a beautiful process and the impending show made me forget temporarily about the visceral conflict going on inside of my being.

The top half of the chamber closed completely encapsulating Fox within it. I could see the calm lifeless body through the see-through panels. Completely closed, Fox's life energy would be trapped and saved. I just now needed to wait until the sensor picked up and stored his energy. I decided I needed to go to the bathroom to splash some water on my face to completely regroup myself.

I hadn't taken two steps before the sensor indicated the life energy had been detected and storage was beginning. It should have taken hours, days in some cases, but it had only been a few minutes; Fox was truly a special specimen. Forgoing the visit to the bathroom, I got right to work on starting the Reincarbonation. The genetic modification had already been programed so it was just now a matter of marrying the new genetic sequence to the life energy.

The energy was collected in record time, and eager to bring the man back, I began the procedure. My heart once more raced, but it wasn't out of fear this time, instead it was excitement. I was doing things through science which once were only thought to be possible by gods. I pressed the button, and chills ran down my back and every hair on my body stood in excited attention.

The body began to glow as the cells were agitated on a quantum dimension. The humming sound started, I still hadn't figured out where it was coming from or how it was happening. It was a beautiful sound nonetheless which is why I really hadn't worried to try to eliminate it. As one parent once described during his son's Reincarbonation, it was the angels singing.

The body kept vibrating and the angels kept singing to me, until the body was no more but an outline made out of pure light and energy. It was like looking at a distant star, it didn't shine or blind but just glowed, while the light danced and rippled. Once proper quantification was achieved, I reintroduced the life energy along with the modification and augmentations for Fox's body.

It was always a beautiful sight when the ethereal and corporal energies met. Colors would erupt and dance through the body, making it look like a psychedelic lava lamp prism. Primary, secondary and colors that didn't even have a name flowed through the body as the soul found its old home. The vibration began to slow down and the outline of colors and light started to look more and more like Fox. Soon the spectacle ended and as always, I wiped away from my face the tears of joy and pride of what I had created.

The monitor came back to life and the slow, calm rhythm of Fox's once more living heart filled the air. His eyes opened, and I opened the top part of the pod and went through the usual protocol question for all Reincarbonated patients; as expected, Fox passed with flying colors.

The presentation to officials and the few politicians in the know was a completely different thing all together. They were impressed with Fox's incredibly augmented senses, but they wanted more, they always wanted more. Fox was the prototype and they wanted to see how far they could really push the technology and humanity.

Time after time after time, I repeated the procedure on Fox, each time with another "tweak" and augmentation of some sort. Through the process, I remember discovering the idea of a totem. I wanted to remember more, but my mind was fighting me. The memories that flashed through my head became more sinister, macabre and bloody.

With each modification and augmentation, Fox was tested, sometimes successfully others ending in grandiose failure. Sometimes I had a whole Fox for the procedure sometimes a body part. A flash of a memory of only placing a hand in the Reincarbonation chamber quickly haunted me. Disjointed pictures and memories kept flowing through my brain of my time with Fox until I latched onto one I wished I never had remembered.

I stormed out of the conference room, slamming the door while still screaming a few vulgarities. All the eyes that I had left inside the room stood wide open in disbelief as they were not used to ever being addressed in such a vile way. I was angry, tired and frustrated. I had spent too much time involved in the development of the Re-Soldier, time I could have used much better finding and helping people who truly needed it.

I also knew they had me by the balls, the money funding this project was on the border of absurd and my personal attention was required all the way through completion. What had been asked of me inside that boardroom was something I never had even imagined nor contemplated. For once they had called check mate on me, and I had no other out than to concede.

I went back to the complex to find Fox testing his newest upgrades. He was like a kid with a new toy every time he came back. While every time I had to put him under, a small part of me died along with him. I pulled Fox into my office and explained to him what I had been "requested" to do. He seemed excited at the challenge and wanted to proceed without delay, while I was still trying to figure out how to get out of it.

I put it off for several days, coming up with every possible reason not to do it, even to the extent of faking illness. Once I could not dodge the phone calls anymore, and after several serious threats of funding being pulled, I had no other recourse but to oblige to the demands. I called Fox into the practicing arena and once more went over with him what had to be done. As a good soldier, he nodded and replied time after time with "Yes, Sir."

They didn't want me to put him under, nor did they want it to be an accident. They required for Fox to go through a possible reality every soldier must accept, and many endure, to be killed. Not to die but to be killed and murdered. Being that Fox and I were the only ones with access to the complex, it was in my hands to do the dirty deed. It had been excruciating putting him under every time. I had endured each time, allowing my curious mind to dive into the advancement and progress we were making. I ignored my soul and screams of my conscience as I took the life of a healthy man over and over again just to make him a better weapon of war. Now I was asked to put a gun to his head, pull the trigger, and then bring him back as if nothing had happened.

Fox stood before me in attention and ready for the next step, as he liked to called them. He was gracious enough to walk me through how to use the sidearm and all its features. I numbly listened to the man instruct me how to place a bullet in his head as if he was giving driving directions. He showed me I was to shoot for maximum lethality and accuracy. He finally handed the pistol to me and it felt cold; the steel felt so incredibly heavy in my hand.

I gripped the gun and took in how it looked grasped in my hand. I kept my finger as far away from the trigger as possible, worried that if I even graced it, the pistol might accidentally go off. Fox stood silently at attention and waited for me to do whatever I needed to do.

Feeling completely disconnected from my body, I slowly began to raise the black pistol towards Fox's head. My right hand was trembling, so I solicited the help of my left hand to steady the gun. The shaking calmed but was still there. I placed and aimed the gun at Fox's temple as he had instructed me. He peaked out of the corner of his eye and corrected my angle of aim. He stood proud and ready, and I trembled like a broken man and a coward. I slowly moved my right pointer finger onto the trigger. The gun was becoming heavier every second I held it up a few inches from Fox's head. My shoulders begun to burn and my hands to shake even more than they already were. I took a few deep breaths and did my best to steady the instrument of death I was holding between my sweaty palms before I slowly began to pull on the thin but menacing trigger.

"Time to move."

I once more jumped at the voice next to me. This time it was Helena. Everyone moved and we started to head down the hill as I fumbled to find a pocket to put my binoculars in. Kate's hand reached out and grabbed them from me. She gave me that all too perfect smile and made the viewing apparatus disappear.

Once we had reached the now red and green lawn, thankfully all of the mess had been cleaned and hidden by the Alpha team. Only five out of the original 9 members of the Alpha team remained and they had taken up posts next to the door. Only their commander stood with us.

"Once we open the door, we will only have twenty minutes until we must retreat back to the transport," said the Alpha team commander.

"I hate to point out the obvious once more, but unless I forgot my math during my last reincarbonation, that only allows us ten minutes in and ten minutes out. We could run around this place for days even if all the schematics are accurate."

"It will be enough time," Helena was nice enough to clear up.

Kate held my hand and tugged at me she smiled and just shook her head, gently warning me not to open my big mouth once again. I hushed and just went along for the kamikaze ride we were about to embark on. We all moved toward the door. I was surprised not to see a single camera or any other re-soldier as far as the eye could see. I guess when your security guard can punch a hole through a man's chest he doesn't need backup often. A scary thought did pop into my head. If this is the perimeter security, what must be like inside?

I pushed that scary but logical thought out of my head as Kate ushered me toward the door where the rest of the team was waiting.

"Everyone ready? 3, 2... 1." The commander opened the door at the end of his countdown, and Helena and Fox went in first. Kate ushered me behind them and D brought up the rear. The door closed after us, and I suddenly felt claustrophobic in the giant building.

There were no gunshots, no one jumped or attacked us. The only thing that snuck up on us were the plumes of warm air exiting our mouth and making tiny little clouds in front of our faces. It was cold, very, very cold inside. I wished someone had warned me, I might have worn a fashionable jacket or a mink coat. Instead I stood there with a chill going down my spine and also incredibly cold.

We stood in an open space and I felt very exposed. To both the left and the right, the pathways seemed to go on forever. The building was well illuminated, but it looked like a warehouse, at least the part we entered. We stood at the cross point of a T made out of metal warehouse racks. The racks were filled with canisters and boxes, all on pallets. They were stacked three levels high, making them feel like walls. Unlike the view to the each side, toward the front, we could only see so far before the skeletal metal walls seemed to twist and turn and cut off our view.

After everyone was satisfied that we were alone, Fox gave some hand signals and the two teams started moving in different directions. Fox and Helena took off toward the right and moved with speed and precision. They seemed very certain of where they were going. I really hope the schematics were accurate for the sake of all of us.

D took the lead, and we started heading straight in into the belly of the massive building; lucky us. Kate and I followed D, and I felt like a Greek champion entering the labyrinth. Only that this one was made of metal racks, pallets and some sort of supplies. D moved fast and Kate and I did our best to keep up. Once we reached the first intersection, without hesitation, D took a left then a quick right. So far so good; I could tell we were moving in the same direction.

The items filling the pallets on the racks kept changing. Everything from what was labeled as "Saline" to metal canisters with poison labels on them. I tried to look and absorb as much as I could as we kept winding our way through the metal maze, but it was too fast and too much to take in at once. By the time I had quit trying to inventory the items on the racks, I had completely lost my sense of direction and was now blindly following D.

D suddenly stopped and motioned us to back ourselves and become one with the metal racks. We had reached the end of the labyrinth and were now looking at what appeared to be proper walls and offices across from where we were. D quickly scanned in both directions, just like his mom must have taught him before crossing the road as a kid, signaled us to remain put and entered the open space between the safety of the maze and the man door before us on the wall. He moved quickly through the span and eventually found the false safety of the white wall across from us. He signaled for us to move toward him. I and Kate ran as fast as our feet would take us toward him.

We hunched by a door which had a now very familiar hand biometric lock. Why we hunched I wasn't certain, would people only notice us only if we stood straight? Would they walk by and say? "Hey, what are those people doing standing nice and tall over there?" Or would they think "Who are those people over there? Oh wait, they are hunching, pay no attention to them." Either way, D motioned for me to use my hand on the biometric panel. I did as he asked, and after a few seconds of scanning and buzzing, the door unlocked in front of us. We quickly darted through it into the unknown perceived safety that lay behind it.

I thought we were entering a room, but the cold building kept playing mind games on me. All three of us stood at the beginning of another corridor. The walls were white and compulsively clean. Each side of the walls of the hallway was lined with doors. Doors ready to release a re-soldier, a worker or even the boogey man himself. The hallway was very well lit, the light bouncing off the perfectly white walls, almost eliminating all shadows. The air had that filtered hospital smell to it, clean and full of possible rare diseases waiting to colonize us. D kept moving forward, stopping and pointing his gun as we passed every staggered door on both our lefts and rights. He kept a fast almost frantic pace as he cleared each door, keeping his military precision but not wasting any second to fear or hesitation.

We continued with our reckless abandon pace, and for the first time, the clock started to tick in my head. It dawned on me that we had been in here for a quite a few minutes, and we only had ten precious minutes each way. Eventually D stopped in front of one of the doors. The door, as all the other doors, was plain and devoid of all frills. It was solid and as a white as the hallway. I could not tell what it was made out of, but it held a sturdiness and heft to it. It stared at us, full of potential and fear; the only things breaking up its pure whiteness were two numbers. A three and three, door thirty-three hid behind it our faith and possibly the faith of millions of people. D motioned me to another hand scanner, and hearing the constant tic-toc in my head now, I put my hand on it as quickly as possible. The familiar buzzing and the unlocking of the door ensued.

Once more, we were through the door quickly, but instead of forging ahead, D stopped dead on his tracks. I looked over his bulging shoulders expecting to find a re-soldier or twenty, instead all I could see was a very large and well-illuminated room with nothing in it. It was perfectly clean, not a single thing inside of it besides the gentle hum of the lights.

For the first time since we entered the building, the confident hulking black man looked completely lost. His weapon was no longer being held up, scanning for possible attackers; instead it was pointed to the ground. After another scan across the large empty room, he took a look at his wrist watch and swung his arm back down in defeat.

"What is the problem, D?" I asked in a hushed voice.

"This is it, this is where it should be, we have arrived and there is not a freaking thing here!" D didn't whisper in a hush tone and his usually friendly tone was replaced by pure hot anger.

We stood there all three of us, Kate holding onto my hand not only to comfort me, but looking for comfort herself. D looking around over and over, as if he kept looking, something might magically appear. We stood there for a few infinite seconds and the tic-toc in my head just kept getting louder and louder. D stopped scanning the room and his left hand went up to his ear.

"Go ahead... Understood, we found the same here...

Affirmative... Shit! Shit, shit, shit, shit... Understood."

# Run for It!

The large man stood there and whatever the conversation he was having didn't inspire much hope in me. Unable to contain myself... "What? What is it?"

D's confused and frustrated look now turned into a furious frown. His eyes held a fire and intensity I had not seen before in them. He looked at me, then at Kate, and then settled his fiery gaze back on me. He looked me in the eyes and without blinking or showing any other emotion but rage; he delivered the overwhelming news to us.

"Nothing adds up. It is a trap and we must go now."

His words came crisp, clear, urgent but still somehow calm. In my head, a million different scenarios began to play out, all of them ending in the gruesome and bloody end of my life. At the same time, the obvious signs began to click and become perfectly clear in how we had ended up here. Only one guard, no backup ever arrived. Our whole way into this room, we had heard voices in the distance but never even been close to encounter a single soul. It had been too easy, and we had walked right into it. Unlike everyone else, my dirty little paws had been letting anyone watching know that I was here. They hadn't interfered so they must have wanted me in here. The question now was. What have we really walked into?

Without any further hesitation, D let us out of the empty room. I had expected a welcoming party of armed men outside in the hallway led by an eye patch-wearing villain ready to give us his "Gotcha" speech, but all there was were the hallways and its clean air. We turned left and ran down the hallway toward our entry door without a concern of what might or might not jump out, out of the many doors that flanked us. As we approached the door back into the labyrinth of a warehouse, gun fire slowed our stride until we reached a full stop yards away from the door. D stood there looking back and forth from where we had come and back to the door we were trying to return to. He did a couple of small little hops like a kid trying not to go to the bathroom, and as the gunfire got louder, he led us away from the exit door.

"That was the way back," I protested as I kept my close pursuit of the muscled islander.

"We cannot go back that way. We don't' have enough bullets to fight our way out, no one does. There are other ways out." He spoke clearly and calmly as I chased at a full sprint after him. His words didn't seem fatigued, as if this was just a stroll for him. Kate held my hand as we ran, and I was impressed with her physical ability and the calmness exuding out of her, even as I felt we were running to our deaths.

We zigged and zagged a couple of times through the hallways filled with numbered doors and white walls. As we moved, pictures were starting to appear on the once empty walls between doors. We were running too fast to really see what was in the framed poster size pictures, and the feeling of being chased by someone or something I hadn't seen yet kept my focus of keeping up with D.

D took a sharp right into a hallway, it was so quick and abrupt, I couldn't make the turn as D did in front of me and Kate. As I stumbled to catch myself and continue down our new route, one of the pictures on the wall didn't only catch my attention but it jumped off the wall and grabbed me.

The picture had two men on the foreground; one was wearing a lab coat, the other a suit. They were shaking hands as the suited man handed some sort of plaque to the other with his left hand. Both men smiled proudly and in the background, a herd of lab coated wearing scientists smiled and tried their best to be captured in the picture without seeming desperate to be in it.

# In the Name of Progress

I found myself in the facility we were running through, but no one was chasing me now. I was entering through what seemed like the facility's main entrance. There were people expecting me as I stepped out of the car that had driven me here. The driver opened the door for me and dozens of unfocused faces enthusiastically shook my hand and thanked me for the honor and visit.

I was ushered through double doors and more welcoming faces and handshakes followed. People kept talking to me, but it was all just murmurs and noise. I knew what they were saying, but I could not make out a single word. Lost in the murmur of the voices, I found myself at a podium, an illuminated screen behind me showing graphs and figures following and changing as I continued to talk. I would stop and people would either laugh or clap, several times getting on their feet to applaud for whatever bit of information I had just divulged or explained to them.

The thunderous applause ended the presentation, one second I was walking down the stage steps waving at the fanatical crowd, the next I was at a table with a succulent bright red lobster sitting in the plate in front of me. A glass full of white wine accompanied the delectable plate, and I could taste every last morsel of sweet lobster meat and the clarified butter in which I dunked the perfectly cooked meat. Conversations were going on around my table and the tables around me. I was part of them; I could feel myself smiling and responding, but the words and the conversation was just like listening to blood rush through your veins as you lay drunk on a bed after a long night of drinking.

Once more I found myself on stage, instead of being behind the security of the podium, I found myself holding the microphone pacing back and forth while rallying the blurry faces in the crowd. A suited man stood across from me, holding his own microphone and a glass of wine. We bantered back and forth until the crowd broke into a thunderous roar of applause. A man was walking up to us, everyone in the crowd looking at him with their eyeless faces. The man walked his way up the side stair of the stage and was now standing between us. More unintelligible words were uttered by me and the suited man, and the crowd hooted, clapped and roared accordingly.

The suited man took a step back and extended his hand out to me and the lab coat wearing man on stage with me. A plaque appeared in my left hand and I smiled in my suit as the flashes blinded us and crowd clapped and cheered in approval. Then man wearing the lab coat shook my hand vigorously and his smile was raw and complete. He thanked me after the lighting storm of flashes, and he gave me a hug. He embraced me and I embraced him back. I felt love and pride for the man in the lab coat, but did not know who he was.

I was being pulled and pried away from the proud man in the lab coat. I fought to stay in his embrace and the pride and love I was feeling, but the tugging and the repeated gentle "Baby" snapped me back into the hallway. The picture still stood before me, the man in the coat smiling, shaking my hand and proudly accepting the plaque I was handing to him while wearing my fancy suit.

# Dirty Laundry

I started to point with my left hand to the picture, my mouth opening trying to explain what I had just seen but unable to utter a sound.

"I know, baby, but we need to move, now, please, baby." Kate was pulling at my right arm and her eyes pulling at my soul to stay with her and to move with her. D was halfway down the new hallway we had entered, shooting back worried and urgent looks to us. I shook off the fog, convinced my feet to move and started chasing after the muscled man.

We ran down the new hallway, and as we have been doing in our panicked run, ignored any of the doors flanking us. Thankfully nothing had jumped out of them and eaten us yet. We reached the end of the corridor and a door once more faced us, this time only silence came through it instead of gunfire. D motioned me towards a hand biometric screen and I obliged. As I moved toward it, I could not help but to be pulled back into my memories. Why was I wearing a suit? Why did it feel so vivid and so recent?

The door unlocked and instead of rushing through it, D paused for a second, looked back at me, and after much searching could only utter one phrase. "I am sorry." His breath made fake smoke in front of him; he turned his back and went through the door.

Even though we have been running for the last few intense moments, I felt colder. The cold smoke was exiting through our noses now, making us look like angry dragons. The temperature fell even more and my skin broke out in goose bumps as we broke the threshold of the new door.

Once more there were metal racks in front of us. Unlike the first ones we encountered, these racks were only one level high and looked more like pens than storage racks. Kate and I, hand in hand, kept moving forward with our focus on keeping up with D. He ran faster than before and I had to use all of my strength to keep up the pace and not let go of Kate's hand. D was keeping an almost unmatchable pace and I struggled to keep up while the cold air made my lungs hurt.

D was forced to take a sharp left and that is when I first noticed the piles inside the racks. It looked like piles of tattered clothes. I took the left and continued after him struggling to keep up. He continued his breakneck pace as we turned again, a pair of boots caught my attention out of the pile. They were military and black like the ones I had borrowed from the locker-room inside the Wall. Down the next hallway between the racks and the pens, D stepped into a puddle and I did my best to avoid but failed, it was full of red liquid grease and it splashed heavy and thick as my boots made their way through it.

More running more turns, every time some other piece of clothing catching my attention. Gloves, pants, jackets, there was a ridiculous amount of clothing piled in these pens and even though I was moving faster than I thought I could, the clothing didn't seem to make sense. I kept seeing boots mixed in with shirts, and jackets mixed in with pants and gloves. Whoever organized this needs to be fired.

Kate started pulling me harder to keep up with her and D, I didn't think this sweet girl could move that fast, but all the times I thought I was pulling her along, I was really just holding her back. As she tugged on me, my body turned a bit counterclockwise and that is when I saw it, a face looking back at me from within of the piles. The unblinking eyes stared at me, the mouth slightly open with speckles of dried blood on it. The eyes stared at me, but they were empty and soulless.

At first I thought it was a re-soldier tracking us down but in my panic I came to an abrupt stop, Kate's hand tried to stay in mine but her momentum and my sudden stop made us break our engage and she kept on drifting forward. I stopped and finally recognized the specific but mysterious smell which had been nagging me since we entered this maze. It smelled like a butcher's shop, the smells that kept calling to me but escaping me were the distinctly sweet and metallic smell of blood.

The smell hit me, and as I stood there searching for the haunting face in the piles, the piles became clear. They were not piles of misarranged clothing items, they were piles of bodies. Dead lifeless bodies and all of their empty accusatory eyes were looking at me. I stood there and the room kept getting bigger and bigger the hallways made by the pens seem to extend as far as my eyes could see in every direction. All of the pens were filled with piles and piles of dead bodies and in some cases just body parts. The bodies, the arms, the legs and the bodiless heads filled the pens, and the pattern of organization finally became clear to me. Different colored uniforms and camouflage seem to be kept together. I stood in an aisle where all the bodies were a myriad of shades of brown and wore green camouflage. As I peeked over the other aisles, more colors of uniforms and more colors of soldiers decorated the bloody ground. I stood there and knew where I was. I didn't have to ask this time. These men and women should be buried somewhere with a monument to remind everyone of their service and sacrifice.

Instead they lay here partially frozen and preserved after their arranged and planned murder. They lay here with the looks they had in their eyes when the re-soldiers turned on them. Their genetic material laid here in tattered piles of bloody and dirty clothing ready to become what ended their short lives. They lay here as soulless vessels ready to be brought back just to obey and kill in the name of the Board.

How where they doing it? How without their life energy? Then I remembered the plaque, the applause, the handshakes and the smiles.

For the first time since we started this mission, I can honestly say to myself I felt the rage and the anger I kept seeing in the others' eyes but could not explain. It burned white and completely inside of me. I knew what horrible existence awaited those souls once they were reincarbonated. I had the overwhelming urge to burn this place down, not only to stop whoever was behind this, but also liberate those poor souls lying in discarded piles in front of me.

Once more Kate started ushering me along, but the pure anger would not let me listen to her or move from where I stood. I slowly started to yield to her attempts to make me advance and rejoined her and D. This was never meant or created to be used like this. Who had taken such a beautiful thing I created and turned it into something so dark, ugly and despicable? More importantly: Why? What is there to gain from this monstrosity?

We ran through more hallways lined with bodies, but I could tell D's usual decisive flow had been altered. He would make a move toward our right, stop and head back towards the opposite direction. At first I thought he might be lost or that like me, the anger had blinded him and made him a little disoriented. After a couple more double take turns, I noticed the first set of eyes. They weren't the same dead eyes that had been watching us as we maniacally ran through the maze of bodies. These eyes were alive and held purpose. They rested inside calm but determined faces and silhouettes of bodies being partially obscured by piles of bodies. As I kept looking around, I spotted more and more of this slow approaching army of re-soldiers in the adjacent and further away halls.

We were no longer trying to navigate our way out of the maze of flesh; we were now trying to escape our pursuers and not become one of the bodies in the stalls. We continued to run with the same urgency as before, but now it was accompanied with panic and fear. We all found another gear we didn't realize we were hiding and ran faster than we had.

Ahead the promise of an exit from the carnage around us flirted with my eyes. There didn't appear to be any more turns ahead, instead a short clearing of a concrete floor then a white inviting hallway. We didn't follow our parent's instruction and checked the left and right before crossing. We darted through the clearing, throwing caution to the wind. As we crossed the span that seemed to never end, re-soldiers were approaching us from both the left and the right. Good thing we didn't look, we might have become paralyzed at the threat surrounding us.

# Hide and Seek

In an unnerving unison, the four re-soldiers to our right and the three to our left uttered a haunting phrase. "Give Him back to us." The words sent chills through my spine and there was no doubt they spoke of me. They uttered it again. "Give Him back to us." Their voices reverberated on each other, making the already terrifying demand, bowel emptying worthy. We ran and I finally felt I wasn't running to hurry, but that I was running for my life. We reached the white hallways and escaped into them and away from the re-soldiers through the opening.

D started trying doors as we progressed through the clean whiteness of the hallway. Each time a defeated grunt came out of the big man and we moved on to the next door. There were no fancy hand scanners for me to work my magic on and even when he tried to either kick or put his shoulder and body into the doors, they would just not yield. After many grunts, kicks and frustration one of the doors decided to provide us asylum, or so we thought.

We entered what appeared to be a laboratory. Four tables and island cabinets dissected the room creating three pathways across from it. On the counters lay Bunsen burners, test tubes, solutions and many other devices I could not remember the name for. The counter tops were pure black, counterbalancing the whiteness of the walls and the brightness of the lights above. There were plenty of colorful stickers giving warnings like poisonous dart frogs on several jars and bottles.

But the real danger stood just ahead down the middle pathway in the room. A re-soldier stood tall strong and determined not to let us continue on our escape. Unlike the one before and more so like the ones I had partially seen through the flesh maze, this re-soldier seem more grotesque. His facial features, although they were composed of the same parts as my face, just did not make sense. His nose seemed too thick, his ears too pointy, his neck seemed to bulge in places it shouldn't, his eyes, oh his eyes were far too sunken into his skull under his over pronounced brow ridge.

I wanted to categorize him as one of the models we see of Neanderthals, but it was more than that. It was animalistic, the sum of the parts of his face might say human but the parts were something else. He stood there, more bulges and muscles rippling through his scared and stretched skin. He looked straight at D and once more the haunting phrase escaped from his lips.

"Give him back to us." His voice deep, thick and held the grumble of a large cat. Without hesitation, D opened fire at the re-soldier before us. The rounds came out fast and loud, the firing machine gun echoed off walls of the laboratory and the noise was deafening. I wanted the noise to end, but having what stood in front of us was absorbing the bullets' impacts and not showing any sign of pain or even awareness it was being shot at, I resigned myself to the possibility of my ears bleeding until I was deaf, and in my head, I rooted for D to continue the barrage of bullets.

The gun clicked empty, and without hesitation, D dropped the machine gun and began a graceful run toward the re-soldier and produced two short machetes out of the black leather holsters he had on each one of his muscular thighs. He pulled them out as he ran toward the re-soldier, and the move looked as if he had performed it thousands of times. It was fluid and graceful while at the same time terrifying and incredibly intimidating. If it had been me, I would have probably cut my leg, managed to cut my belt, had my pants fall down to my ankles and impaled myself to death with the machete on the other hand.

The re-soldier stood there, allowing the hulking islander to rapidly charge at him. He stood there and not a single drop of fear could be spotted on his face. It was as if all the bullets had just bounced off of him. As the clash became inevitable, the re-soldier shifted, moving his right foot back and raising his hands in a martial arts type of stance. The problem was that his hands were not hands, they were claws. I don't mean he needed a manicure, I mean they were claws like that of a lion or a tiger. Five fingers, but yea freaking claws!

D had closed the distance between them and started swinging and rotating his short machetes, making the re-soldier move while swatting away at the machetes to defend himself. Even though it didn't seem to possess fear, at least I knew it had the need for self-preservation. A graceful dance of steel and claws ensued, both attacking and both successfully defending themselves.

They both moved with a speed and agility that was hard to follow with my own two eyes and standing not more than ten yards from them. The first hit was landed by the re-soldier, four tears appeared on D's black shirt, exposing the four crimson lines ruining his perfect muscles. D twinged at the strike, but it didn't seem to slow him down. The faster than the eye dance continued in front of me and Kate. They leapt and moved urgently but gracefully around each other. In one of the machete pirouettes, the blade struck down and instead of the clawed hand redirecting the blow, the clawed hand ended up lying on the floor. The re-soldier didn't show any sign of pain or of being affected by his now missing appendage. The re-soldier continued to fight and surprisingly very little if any blood seemed to be exiting his body from the stump where his claw once was.

D continued the fighting, not taking any time to celebrate his small victory. The re-soldier's urgency increased and he became more violent, sensing that he might actually not come out ahead on this fight. D was struck by re-soldier's handless arm and it sent him flying toward the wall. He hit the wall solidly and I expected him to hit the ground like a sack of potatoes, pass out and leave me and Kate alone to deal with this now angry re-soldier.

The big man hit the wall hard, his body made the sound a hand makes when one tries to kill a mosquito sucking the blood out of your leg. It was solid but held that reverberation that only meat and flesh can make. To my joy and surprise, he landed gracefully on one knee with both of his blade wielding hands resting on the ground. He looked back up at his foe from this kneeling position and charged him. The machetes were moving so fast and so relentlessly through the air, they were impossible to keep track of with the naked eye. The speed was frenetic and endless, and even though you could not quite see the moving blades, you could certainly hear them as they cut and displaced the air as they moved through it.

D's movements were now angry and precise; I would have not wanted to be on the other end and see that coming toward me. It was like helicopter blades rapidly approaching my soft fleshy body, ready to tear it to pieces. Unlike me, the re-soldier stood there prepared and without fear. As D reached the re-soldier, he moved avoiding the failed strike from the re-soldier then proceeded to take his turn accosting the injured re-soldier. D swung the short machete with his right hand and the re-soldier deflected the blow, spinning D. He spun and continued his attack using the force of the deflection. D attempted a strike with his left blade, and as the re-soldier once again defended his second spinning attack, D then brought his right hand around and trusted the blade through the re-soldier's torso.

Time had slowed down for me, whether it was the adrenaline pumping through me or I had rediscovered some modification in my genetic code from the reincarbonation, I was not sure. But I could see every flexion of the muscles, the blades slowly moving through the air and the droplets of sweat and blood gently dripping out of both of them

The sound had vanished from my ears not being able to keep up with my eyes until the blade made a wet and solid noise as it entered the body of the re-soldier right in the middle of his torso just under the sternum. Although the blade was short, it made it all the way through the re-soldier's back, the rounded shiny metal tip of the machete showing and covered in crimson blood. The re-soldier gasped as his eyes met D's, without hesitation D cocked his left arm across and above his body, and in one fell swoop separated the re-soldier from his head. D placed a boot on the headless torso of the re-soldier, pried out his blade, gave them both a quick wipe on his pants and placed them back in their leathery homes.

The muscled islander turned his attention back to us as we stood there mouths open in amazement at what we had just witnessed. "We must keep moving."

# Red Mist

I nodded like a bumbling idiot who tried to close my mouth before a fly flew in and followed him, Kate in tow, toward the other side of the room which the headless re-soldier once guarded. I was amazed and intimidated by what I had just witnessed and knew that the faith in my security which I had placed in D was well merited.

We went through the next set of doors and out of the laboratory just to find ourselves in an adjacent laboratory room but just bigger. We entered the room and the same four rows of laboratory benches were displayed in front, as in the previous room. Again all sorts of equipment, tools and fire making metal tubes were sprawled all over the tables. This room was longer and the tables only went so far before they ended, intersected by bisecting hallways. This happened three more times, making the room look like a big four by four grid.

Also unlike the other room, instead of one re-soldier staring at us from the opposing door, there stood seven of them. Three of them in the last hallway of the grid each of their imposing and cold figures filling each pathway, denying us exit from the room. Two of them were to our left, one each per pathway; the other two mirrored the ones on the left but to our right. We were being presented with a frontal force while being flanked on both sides also. All of the doors out of the grid-like laboratory room were covered by the re-soldiers.

I instantly thought of going back the way we came, but D took a step forward toward the sentinels guarding the pathways. Either he had a death wish or our only way out was forward. All seven re-soldiers at once uttered "Give Him back to us." The phrase just kept getting creepier and creepier every time I heard it, and no matter how nice or how many times they asked, I had no desire to be in their company.

D's hands once more wielded his two short machetes, his forearms flexing and squeezing the handles of the blades, preparing himself for a severely handicapped fight. I foolishly tried moving forward to join in the fight, I felt like I would rather die fighting than going back with the re-soldiers. Kate grabbed me as I tried to move forward and thwarted my plans of a glorious Viking battle death.

I stood there, Kate holding onto my right arm for her safety and to prevent my foolishness when the three swooshing noises and three clicks grabbed my attention. The noise came from the other side of the room and behind the re-soldiers. There was a swoosh, a click, a thud, and it repeated two more times. The three re-soldiers across from us gently jerked, and one by one from right to left, there was a loud bang and they disappeared one by one. All that was left was a gentle red mist slowly floating back to the floor.

Through the falling mist of blood, Helena stood firmly holding her weapon. I have never been so glad to see a pair of braids. I had witnessed D being a badass a few moments earlier, but I thought even his badassness had limits and seven re-soldiers might be it.

"MOVE!!!" was the only thing the muscular woman screamed at us as she opened machine gun fire towards the re-soldiers on our right. Fox appeared from behind her and opened fire on the re-soldiers on out left. D had sheeted his blades and somehow was behind us ushering, well pushing me along as Kate tugged me toward Helena and Fox. D had pulled out a handgun and all three of them were shooting bullet after bullet, changing their magazines and continuing with the rain of bullets at the four remaining re-soldiers; Helena and Fox from the front and D from behind us to which ever re-soldier seemed to be advancing the most toward us.

We crossed the span of the room, crossing through the mist of blood, cautious not to slip on the puddles left where the re-soldiers once stood, and once more we were deafened by the incessant firing of the guns. We made it through the door Fox and Helena were guarding for us and out into another hallway. D instantly went to into hyperaware mode scanning back and forth with his handgun in the hallways. Helena and Fox were slowly backpedaling without looking back to the door. They kept the firing going until they were able to walk out of the doorway shutting and locking the door behind them.

Helena took the point and led us to our left in our brand new hallway. Fox caught up to her and D brought up the rear, we were back in our apparent standard formation with me and Kate protected in the middle. We made a few twists and turns through the hallways, and no one jumped out of any door, and any time I looked back, I didn't see anyone in hot pursuit of us.

We had been confronted twice and had been followed through the maze of bodies, they knew we were here and they had to know exactly where we were, but none of the re-soldiers seemed to want to get too close. And to truly think of it, I don't believe they had started an attack yet. Maybe they were more scared of us and just wanted us out. Maybe we were the humans and they were the mouse. Even though we were scared of the little mouse, they were more scared of us and hid until we were out of sight.

And then we took a right, and half way through the hallway, I realized we were the mice and we had fallen right into their sticky trap.

As we ran through the hallway, our boots echoing and thundering, in front of us the view went from open hallway to a solid mass of re-soldiers. They poured out of the doors and made a wall of bodies impeding our progress.

Helena yelled, "Back, back!"

We did an about face and started heading back from where we had come. My heart sunk as another wall of bodies started to spill out of the doors we had previously passed. We were cornered, we were more than cornered, we were stuck and trapped, and I felt like a poor little mouse squealing and struggling in the glue trap for his life.

Once again, the creepy chant came from both sides of us and in stereo. "Give Him back to us." If I make out of this alive, I am making that chant into a song, apparently it is catchy. I will make a killing selling it to re-soldiers. I didn't think my career in the catchy music business was going to be a success nor was I getting out of this alive. Right now I was hoping Helena and Fox had set the explosives and I would go out in the domino effect explosion. I would rather go out that way than being handed back to this unnerving army.

They slowly started to march toward us from both directions, further cornering us and making my newfound claustrophobia act up once more. Every one of us stood there studying what little options we had. To our right, a small army of re-soldiers and to our left another small army of re-soldiers, slowly approaching. Could we shoot and fire out way out? Did Helena have more of those red mist making rounds on her? Did she have enough?

From my guardians' body language and desperate looking around for another way out, I took the answer to all those questions was a big fat NO. Great, next options. Two doors remained close enough to where we could make a run to them. Two doors held the possibility of salvation, one down the left and one down the right. It would mean we would have to temporarily charge one of the re-soldier small armies to reach the door and hope we could kick, shoot or explode our way through it. Of course, all the while not knowing what lay behind them. Two doors, what could they hold within them? Would we find safety, or would we find an even larger group of re-soldiers waiting for us, or would we get lucky and find a brand new car to drive ourselves out of this mess?

Left or right, right or left? The marching continued and the hallway kept getting smaller. Decisions, decisions, decisions. To my utter dismay, we chose both. I had heard of divide and conquer, but I was pretty sure they had the numbers on us.

"D, take them two and head to that door. Me and Fox will head to the other." Helena barked the orders and before I could protest, she shot me a glance and took off with Fox toward the door down the right, opening fire on the re-soldiers as they charged them. D took off on the other direction as instructed, and Kate pulled me along behind him as my mouth was opened and in the middle of a "What the fuck?!" Thankfully D opened fire at the re-soldiers we were now running toward, instead of away from and it drowned my cursing from Kate's gentle ears.

# Secrets Behind the Door

We were moving so I moved as is my life depended on it, because it did. D kept laying cover fire shooting at the re-soldiers we were approaching as they continued their slow march toward us. Their pace seemed to increase as they saw us approaching the door. We were almost to the door, they were getting dangerously close, and we still didn't know if the door would open. D ran just past the door and went on to change his magazine just to find out he was out. No more cover fire for us. From behind us, I could hear both Helena's and Fox's guns still firing away. Lucky them I thought to myself.

D dropped his handgun and once more pulled out his two sharp metal friends and readied himself for the worst. I reached the door and it opened, the damn thing opened!!!! I turned the nob and it turned along with my hand. I felt an incredible relief immediately followed by dread of what might be on the other side of the door. I did the only thing I could do and I pushed the door open. There was no army of re-soldiers waiting for us; unfortunately neither was there a new car to make our grand escape in.

I ushered Kate through the doorway as I heard the first noise of steel on flesh next to me. I turned to see and two of the re-soldiers had broken rank, ran to us and D had engaged them. One had the same type of claw hands we had seen earlier. The clawed hands moved through the air trying to strike at D while deflecting and avoiding the strikes from the small machetes. The other re-soldier's hands were, well they weren't hands. He only had three "fingers" and they were honest to god talons. The skin of his hand was especially wrinkly and unnatural and his three long fingers were crowned by three talons almost as long as the fingers themselves. They were also flying through the air striking and swatting at D. The talons were terrifying and could probably gut a man with one swoop, which made me wonder how that poor guy could ever pick his nose, amongst other things.

Prying myself away from my biomechanical questions, I moved on forward. As I went through the door, one of the talons found its way onto D's arm. It cut through his muscles, blood instantly spurting running down his arm and leaving a large wound, giving a peak to the white bone deep in his thick arms. A scream escaped the muscled islander as the machete on his now limp left arm hit the ground making a distinct clinking metal sound.

My eyes followed his blood soaked arm down to the floor to where his trusty blade now lay covered in its master's blood instead of the enemies. Another scream brought my attention back to my protector; he was now leaning on the wall facing the doorway where I now stood frozen and four red gashed now decorated his upper chest and neck. Our eyes met and I could see in his eyes he knew he was not making it out of that hallway. The stare seemed to last a lifetime, and in the slow moving world, the two re-soldiers kept slashing and cutting Demetrius. He stood there holding my gaze, and he just smiled at me as blood started to spurt out of his mouth turning his teeth red as he continued his comforting smile. He kicked the machete over toward me, which rested on the floor by his feet, and as the re-soldiers kept attacking his body, he mouthed the words "Go, Mon." I nodded while still smiling at him, I owed him that. His body began to crumple behind the re-soldiers, so I bent down to grab the machete Demetrius had kicked over toward me. When a man gives his life for you, you use his name and you make sure you remember it for the rest of your life.

As I bent over to grab the blood soaked blade, one of the re-soldiers turned its attention towards me and struck. Kate jumped out of the doorway to shield me. I could hear the tearing of the clothes on Kate's back as the re-soldier struck. She then pushed me into the room closed and locked the door behind us. I stumbled back and did a sort of a backwards somersault, being mindful not to gut myself with Demetrius's machete and safely found my way onto my feet.

I looked around ready to defend myself. There was a desk with an office chair behind it toward my left. The room walls were painted a light grey and decorated with paintings and pictures. To my right, there were some comfy looking chairs with a coffee table in front of them. Plants were scattered and perfectly placed throughout the waiting room type office. I turned and only one other door broke the walls around us. It was a beautiful wooden door, large enough for a giant to walk through, yet classy and delicate.

"Vincent."

I turned back to where Kate was still leaning on the now locked door. In the midst of the classy décor I had forgotten she got struck. I started to rush toward her to make sure she was alright, but she snapped at me to stay put.

"Vincent, there is more that I have to tell you, there is so much more." Her voice gently grew as she kept taking slow methodical steps out of the relative darkness of the entryway. The room was well illuminated, but instead of the bright laboratory and factory lights that lit the rest of the building and left little room for shadows, this room had warm yellow lights. Through the shadows of the entryway, Kate slowly walked toward me. Her body didn't seem right, but I could not place my finger on what was wrong with it. Once she walked into the warm yellow glow of the room, I was flabbergasted that I had missed it and for what I was seeing.

Kate's shirt was ripped and inside her ripped right sleeve her right arm was completely missing. No blood ran down the side of her body, soaking her in crimson. Instead a white thick substance barely had made its way out of where an arm once hung. Her body had been cut from just mid clavicle down to her ribs, she was missing more than just her arm, she was missing a small part of her torso. Still there was no blood. I kept looking desperately for the blood and her flesh, denying myself what my eyes were actually seeing.

After much denial of what stood in front of me, I had to accept what I saw. Instead of flesh and bone exposed from her dismembering wound, all that was there were shinny bits of jagged metal. Instead of blood running down the side of her body, the white thick fluid was seeping out of her exposed metal body. She looked at me and gave me that too perfect smile, not showing a single ounce of pain.

"Please, Vincent, lower the machete. Take a seat, baby, before it all comes flooding back."

I hadn't realized my right hand was not only holding the bloody machete, but was also raised and ready to strike the approaching metal girl. She raised her left still functional arm and kept slowly approaching me, still smiling.

"Please, baby, sit. Please sit before you pass out."

Not only had I seen re-soldiers with apparent animal parts for hands dismember a man, who in a single night, had already saved me a few times. Not only had I walked through a warehouse full of dead soldiers stacked for further use like plastic bottles at a recycling facility. And not only had I signed up to kill hundreds of thousands of reincarbonated soldiers to "save" everyone from the Board. No apparently that wasn't enough. Now I had a redhead made of metal trying to calm me while the only thing I can look at is her half exposed metal entrails while she oozed out some white goop. I had had about enough of this so I stood there and refused to sit. I obviously didn't have much control or knowledge of what was going on, but this bit I could control. I could refuse to sit and I could stand, yes that little much of control over this crazy night I could have. I will stand here, I will hold this bloody short machete and I will take control over everything going on around me.

That is when I felt my ears starting to get warm; the warmth grew out of them as if someone had placed hot coals on them. The warmth grew, spreading first to the back of my head then slowly wrapping forward, finally meeting from both directions on my nose. My vision begun to get blurry and black walls formed around the edge of my vision. The warmth began to extend to my stomach and I felt suddenly nauseous. The walls on the side of my peripheral vision begun to slowly creep in on me as Kate became blurry in front of me and the room slowly and impossibly swayed in front of me. The black walls grew and became a tunnel and what I could see became smaller and smaller. It was like looking through the binoculars once again. I heard the machete make the same distinct sound I had heard it make when it fell out of Demetrious's hands. I looked over to my raised right hand through my binocular vision to find my hand empty, the warmness overtook me. Apparently my control was short lived.

I heard one final "Baby" as what little I could see from out of my tunnel went from my hand to the celling and darkness overtook me as I hit the ground.

# Crashing Waves of Reality

The sounds of waves breaking back and forth played outside my closed eyes, that gentle and heavenly sound. I could feel my back starting to itch from me leaving it exposed to the sun during my impromptu nap. I lay on my stomach as I opened my eyes with my head tilted to my right. Out of my right eye, I could only manage to squint, the sun trying to blind it. My left eye shielded by my own head and nose could see the other sunbathers laying on the sand and kids playing with a Frisbee by the shore.

The sunbathers were scattered on the sand like red speed bumps lying on colorful towels. All of the sunbathers seemed to be enjoying the peace and rhythmic sounds from the sea. The kids were defying gravity while using the ocean as a safety net in their extreme Frisbee game. One kid would throw the disc a little toward the water, and the other would run full bore and dive to catch it, allowing the soft break of the waves to break his fall.

The sand was beautifully white and clean. The palms rustled in the wind and seagulls faintly squawked in the distance, periodically breaking up the rhythm of the waves. I gently raised myself onto my elbows while still lying on my stomach. To my left in a red two-piece bikini and glistening from the copious amount of sunblock and the sun was her. She was lying on her back, wearing oversized sunglasses looking like some sort of mad scientist experiment between a human and a bee. The sunblock was slowly losing its battle against the rays of the sun as her skin was starting to turn red. She turned her sweet beautiful face towards me, her eyes still hiding behind the big black of orbs of her glasses.

"Good morning, sleepy head" She greeted me with a smile and continued to poke at me. "Lunch a little too exhausting for you, handsome? You needed to sleep it off?"

I gave her a devilish smile, picked her slippery body up and ran her all the way to the shore as she squealed and threatened me with various acts of violence. My feet found the water and her threats became more serious and grave. I kept smiling and ran us both into the ocean. Well I ran in, and I threw her into the water as her feet rapidly wiggled and kicked during her airborne journey and an adorable little girl high pitch squeal filled the air.

I kept moving toward her as she broke the surface, smiling but indignant. Her right hand moved to her face, "You are lucky I didn't lose my glasses!" I kept approaching her, now with an even bigger grin on my face. She proceeded to punch me on the shoulder with angry furrowed brows but with a smile betraying her tough look.

The sweet redhead embraced me, our bodies pressed so tight against each other than even the salty waves could not find a space between us. She kissed me passionately and I kissed her back. The world disappeared as our lips and bodies embraced, I was engulfed by pure bliss. After a few perfect moments, the kiss ended and the sun begun to shine again and the back and forth of the sea once more filled my ears as we swayed in the water.

"You are lucky this is our honeymoon," said Kate as she punched me one more time for good measure. "Take me to our room, hubby," she giggled as she said hubby and I obliged to her flirty request. I stood from the floating crouch I was in inside the water and turned with her hand in my right hand as we walked back toward the beach.

I was then walking down the sidewalk into a beautiful home. It was a brisk autumn day, all the tress were a million shades of orange, brown and red. The sun shone brightly overhead and was the only thing that broke the infinity of the crisp blue sky. The wind blew in gusts, each one of them reminding me that I didn't wear enough clothing for the day and making the walk towards my front door seem even longer.

The Victorian house stood large and inviting but still with an edge of mystery to it. It was our first real home and large enough to start a family. It had square, rectangular and round windows and the one cone-shaped peak on one side gave it the feel of a castle. Inside we had remodeled and opened up the floor plan while still keeping the charm of the old house and even building in some secret rooms for the hopefully kids to come.

As I reached the door and was fumbling cold keys in frozen hands, the door opened before me and there she stood smiling, the one thing I wanted to see after another crazy day of work. Kate's smile beamed at me and she pulled me into the house, gave me a passionate kiss, making me momentarily forget about the cold.

"Just in time, baby. Just got done with dinner, you had me worried you wouldn't make it home once more."

"We are getting close to a major breakthrough. Tonight I got lucky. We need to let things sit and wait until tomorrow and then check the results."

She was now down the hallway and was starting to bring dishes to the table. I walked down the corridor to her and into the dining room. As she put down the lasagna dish on the table, I gently grabbed her around the waist and pulled her body into mine. Her hands rested on my arms clinched around her waist and her head tilted a little away from me, inviting me to kiss and nibble on her neck.

As I was indulging the sweet and gentle skin on her neck and was determined to kiss her gently until she could not resist the tickles anymore she asked, "When do I find out what this top secret thing you are working on is, baby? I have been very understanding, but between the secrecy and the late nights and even the nights you don't come home at all, I am starting to wonder if there is really a project or if there is just another woman."

I could feel her body tense as she said it and it broke my heart.

That night as I enjoyed her homemade lasagna, I told my sweet Kate about the reincarbonation project. She sat there and listened to every single word I told her. I could see in her eyes how she was trying to not only understand everything I was telling her, but also accept it.

Once I was done with my two servings of lasagna and telling my sweet Kate about what I was doing, she sat there pensive and trying to process the buckets of information I had just given her. She looked down at her lap and after a few moments she said the only thing she could get out at that time and an absolute truth.

"This will change the world," as she said it and how she said it made me wonder if she meant it as good or bad change. I guess I had been wondering that myself all along.

I told my sweet wife thank you for the delicious dinner and chastised her for not eating it herself as she was too busy listening to me, to eat more than a few bites. I stood up from the chair to take our plates back to the kitchen as I heard the voice of the nurse call, "Mr. Rivera."

I stood and walked from the hospital waiting room chairs towards the door guarded by the nurse. She was a short thing in her late 40's with short blonde hair, glasses and very colorful shoes worn below her boring blue scrubs. She did her best to hold a neutral expression on her face, but the desperation and sorrow on my face made her try to give me a comforting smile.

"This way, Mr. Rivera." The nice nurse led me down the main hospital corridor. We reached large double doors and she used the badge she had on her hip on the grey box on the wall. The little grey box made a beeping sound, a light flashed and the doors opened. The door on the left opened toward us, the one of the right into the next hallway that awaited us.

As we kept walking, I could not hold myself back anymore. "How is she?"

"She is stable, Mr. Rivera. Once we get to her room, the doctor will fill you in on all the details."

She said it kindly and in a sweet tone of voice, but also letting me know that it was all she could say. I followed the nurse with the bright pink shoes through a few more hallways until she slowed her pace and walked me into Kate's room.

Kate laid on the bed, she was in her late 30's now, and she looked asleep but as soon as she heard us, she turned her face toward us, greeting me with that smile. I instantly went to her and held her. I hugged and kissed her over and over again. Giving her every kiss I never had had the chance to give her, finally finishing with my mouth resting on her forehead as I caressed her hair with my left hand.

"Baby."

I didn't respond, I just stayed were I was enjoying her, letting the feel of her skin on my lips make the world disappear for me second. Only that this time it didn't, my mind was filled with every possible horrible scenario that might be happening with my Kate.

"Dr. Rivera." The doctor's deep voice broke me out of my macabre trip I was going through in my head. I stood and turned to face the doctor. He was an older man with white hair, glasses and wearing the traditional white coat one comes to expect a doctor to wear. He had a beard and it was as perfectly white as his full head of hair. He stood there holding his chart with kindness in his eyes.

I stood by Kate, my right hand firmly clenching her hand as she lay there looking so helpless on the bed. I prepared myself for the worst while I was already trying to figure out solutions for it. I discovered reincarbonation, I can fix anything, I thought to myself. Then the doctor told me what the problem with my Kate was and then she broke my heart.

"Dr. Rivera, I am Doctor Morton and I have been treating your wife since she was admitted earlier tonight." I had been at work once more and I could not be disturbed. My Kate had been in the hospital now for four hours by herself, I had been too busy to check my phone. Once I decided to check what all the beeping was about, I felt like the world's worst husband. At least I was here now, that had to count for something. Right?

Dr. Morton continued, "Your wife was brought in by ambulance under much duress." Yea, world's shittiest husband I thought to myself. "Her symptoms were numerous and almost seem unrelated. We have spent the last three hours running a multitude of tests on your wife and trying to pinpoint what her ailment is."

The doctor paused as if with even his years of experience and the many times he must had delivered horrible news to relative, it still pained him. "Dr. Rivera, we found that your wife has a very advanced liver cancer." I thought, no big deal, clone her a new liver and good as new, but the doctor decided to keep pilling it on. "Along with her liver cancer, your wife is also suffering kidney failure. She suffered a mild heart attack caused by a blood clot formed on her leg by a cancerous mass she has on her calf. Unfortunately her cancer is very aggressive and has also moved into her spinal column and brain. I am sorry to inform you, as I was sorry to inform your wife earlier, that she is beyond treatment. The best we can do is keep her comfortable"

"How... How is this possible?" My eyes were full of anger directed at the innocent doctor. I did not dare look back at Kate, as long as I didn't look at her, this was still not real and I could fix it. "She was fine this morning when I left the house. How are you telling me this is all happened over the course of the day? Your tests must be wrong, doc!" I said to the doctor with anger and disdain, the old professional allowed me to get everything I needed to get off of my chest and then calmly explained it to me, every careful and gentle word he said broke a little piece of my heart. Every word until I felt there was none of it left.

"Dr. Rivera, as I said your wife came in by ambulance and unresponsive. The preliminary test showed her troponin levels were elevated, this is a telltale sign of a heart attack. As we ran more tests, we stumbled onto other evidence which usually indicates cancer. As we dug and ran body scans and more blood work, we unfortunately came to the diagnosis I gave you, Dr. Rivera. Your wife is still at risk of further heart attacks, and with the aggressive advancement of her cancer, surgery is out of the question; also, other methods to suppress it would just deteriorate her quality or life while not extending her life expectancy."

"Life expectancy?!" Kate's hand tightened around mine as she felt my body want to go confront the poor old doctor in a physical manner. I felt the calm she always gave me, and even without looking back at her, I felt her love for me. I calmed myself as much as I could as hot tears started to roll down my cheeks.

"Dr. Rivera, I am saddened to tell you this and to have had to tell your wife as well. We only give her between six months to one year." The doctor stood there quietly recognizing that news like this is hard to instantly process. But his silence opened my ears to everything else. I could hear the gentle beeping of Kate's heart on the monitor, assuring me she was still there with me. I could hear the oxygen machine rhythmically pumping fresh air into my Kate, helping her breathe. I could hear a mumbled page out in the hallway as some other doctor got summoned to another patient, hopefully not to give them the same kind of news I was just hearing. Finally I could hear, "Baby."

I turned and looked at the sweet redhead laying on her now death bed. Hot tears of anger and denial were still uncontrollably streaming down my cheeks and gently landing on the lapel of my suit. Her beautiful blue eyes looked back at me and a sweet smile tried to provide me comfort, as if I were the broken one.

"It is okay Baby, I am okay with it. You will be okay." OKAY with it? How can I be okay with it? How can I just be okay? I had shared most of my life with this woman: from my first week in college when I arrived as a prodigious fourteen-year-old and she was the only one who offered me friendship. To our first date and kiss at the pizzeria we still frequent when we want a trip down memory lane. Half pepperoni half cheese and two grape sodas, I still remember the order. I remember walking her back to her apartment, me being sixteen, she twenty and feeling like such a hotshot for being out on a date with an older college woman. I remember opening the door for her apartment building and she giving me a sweet gentle kiss on my lips.

How could I just be okay? I remember our first grown up date, taking her to a fancy restaurant; she old enough to order wine and sneaking me some when the waiter walked away. I remember our wedding; her hair looking more red and vibrant that it ever had while she was clad in all white. I remember saying until death do us part, but I never expect death to be this soon.

I would not be okay. I remembered our home, our little family, everything I worked so hard for as she always supported me and kept me organized even when I would forget my name from exhaustion. I could just not be okay with this. I could fix this and I must fix it.

I saw the body of the woman I loved in front of me on her hospital bed, but I could still see the young girl who kissed me while I held the door of her apartment building. Just as in love as I felt that first night and every night and day I had the luck to spend with her. My tears stopped escaping my eyes as I knew I could fix this. Not only had I discovered and perfected the process to fix this, but I could make it happen.

I sat next to her on the bed, still firmly holding her left hand in my right. I gently caressed her forehead and she closed her eyes and smiled. I held and enjoyed that moment as long as I could, how beautiful she looked even here and how my love for her was stronger than ever.

"I can fix this, Kate. This is exactly the type of special case we look for to help with the reincarbonation process. I know the other members of the Board will be in accordance with me and we can get you fixed up sooner than you can get tired of the hospital food here." I smiled at her as hope had filled my heart. Hope that I knew I could fix my Kate and hope of many more nights and even more kisses with my sweet bride.

"I will call an emergency meeting tonight, get the other members of the Board together and probably be ready to start you process tomorrow. Hell if you want, we can take your body back to thwenty-eight instead of thirty-nine, if you want of course." I laughed and the laugh filled the room, she gave me that same frowny smile she had given me in the water at our honeymoon and a million more times since, because she knew the suggestion was as much more for my benefit than it was for hers.

I was shaking her arm and hand gently in the excitement that this was all but a little hurdle in our lives and that by tomorrow, or at the latest the day after, our family would be back to normal. I didn't have to be okay, I didn't have to be oayk with it; I could fix it.

The frown left her brow and the smile her mouth. Her face turned serious, the same serious I had seen a thousand times when she had to give me bad news or when I really messed up. I kept my joyful smile and excitement since this was just temporary. "Why aren't you smiling, sweetie? By tomorrow, Kate this will be just a bad dream, be happy my love."

She smiled at me and my excitement, but the somberness never left her eyes.

"Baby, I can't."

"You can't what, Kate? Be excited? I know, I am sorry I am such an ass, I know today has been hell and you are probably scared, too. But it will be over soon, and you will be back as new, hell better than new."

"No, Baby, I can't. I won't do the reincarbonation." As my heart fell to the floor, every emotion possible rushed through me along with a million questions. All I could muster to say without me breaking down in tears and collapsing was...

"Why not? We need you."

She pulled me toward her, guiding my face onto her chest and I cried, I cried every tear I had and would ever have. I sobbed on top of her as she lay on her deathbed, but still as always, she consoled and supported me. I uncontrollably wept as she caressed my head and sweetly repeated over and over. "Baby, you will be okay."

I slept that night with my Kate in her hospital bed; snuggled close and tight as we had once done many a night back in the small college dorm beds. Tear after tear kept sprouting out of my eyes until I fell asleep. That night I cried every tear I had and have never cried since. That night as I got the most awful news of my life, something inside of me died.

I woke up the next morning still cuddled up with Kate in her hospital bed. I had hoped to wake in our house, in our bed and that all of this had been a guilt-ridden dream. The reality of the conversation between tears from the previous night hit me once more. We talked, we argued, I assured her it was the right choice and we fought over the effects on our family. I tried every argument I could come up with, but she would not relent.

"Baby, it is my time. We need to accept that, you need to accept that." Her words held such finality and firmness to them. Barring drugging her and doing the reincarbonation process then, she was not going to yield, not this time, no matter how relentless I was.

As the weeks passed, at least she agreed to let me set her up in a nicer private room. The other Board members visited her and tried to convince her to go through the procedure out of their own initiative. But like me, they only ran into the resolve and stubbornness about the situation from the feisty redhead.

As the months passed, less and less of my Kate was left on that bed. I stayed strong and didn't shed one more tear. I took a leave from the project and spent my every waking second besides her, caring for her and our family One hundred and forty nine days from the day I had learned my Kate would die, she fulfilled her promise.

We were snuggling in her bed together; she was so much thinner and frail than she ever had been. It was midafternoon and we always took a nap together then. Well she napped, I held her and watched her slee.p I wanted to enjoy every second I had left with her. She kissed me, told me she loved me, and she fell asleep in my arms. She never woke up.

There was no funeral, there was just a trip back to that beautiful beach, me and a canister filled with my Kate's ashes. As I strolled down the beach looking for the perfect spot to lay my Kate to rest, the lovers and couples on the beach reminded me of that one amazing honeymoon and all the trips we took back there. What faith awaited all those couples enjoying each other on the beach? Will they grow old together as I had pictured me and Kate so many times? Or will they be coming back here, broken and empty one day like I was in this moment. I found the spot where I had once thrown her into the sea, and I once more threw my Kate into the sea. I walked out fully clothed into the surf, numb and broken. I opened the canister and gently started to pour my Kate's ashes out of the simple silver urn. The wind billowed the ashes, making a small cloud of her, and after a final goodbye, the wind and the sea took my Kate and I could never have her back. I stood there and not a tear fell, I had no more tears to give my Kate. I stood there in the water until the sun set, reliving every second I had with her, every second I wasted with her and every moment I wished I could have back with her.

I stood there until the beach was deserted and the moon shone brightly overhead. My body shivered from the now cold water and cool night breeze. I stood there, not knowing where to go or what to do. What was there to do without my Kate? I stood there, considering joining her in the sea. As I stood there in the dark water, the wind blew and in the wind I heard. "Baby." I walked out of the cold water uncontrollably shaking and I went home like she would have wanted me to.

# Back to Business

I woke up back in the waiting room office, and Kate was kneeling over by me waiting for me to come back, too. As soon as I saw her face, I shot up, hugged and held on to her as if my life depended on it. I had my Kate, all was well in the world. Every memory I ever had with her came rushing to me and was playing in my head as I held on to her.

Eventually the sad reality of what had happened struck me and I was paralyzed in my hug. I waited there still, as if I had been hugging a hungry bear by mistake and if I moved, I would be its next dinner. I quickly let go of her and started pushing myself back away from her, scooting on my butt. Her expression didn't change at my hot and now cold reaction toward her. I kept scooting back until my back hit the wall and I could not get any further away from her. I lifted my right hand expecting the machete to be there, but I ended up making a cheerleader motion with my empty fist. I was breathing rapidly staring at the one armed metal replica of my dead wife.

"Baby, please calm down. We cannot afford for you to pass out again. We still need to find a way out of here."

Anger cleared my mind and made all approaching dizziness scram away, good ol' fashioned anger to the rescue. "You are dead! My Kate is dead and you are not her; what are you? Who are you?"

Metal Kate smiled and gently nodded. "You are right, baby, I am not her". I had to cut her off as she seemed to be continuing with her explanation.

"Do not call me that. Do not call me Baby. Only she could call me baby and you are but a lie."

"Okay, Vincent, as you wish. As I was going to explain, we do not have the appropriate time for this conversation right now, but I can see you need and deserve some explanation if we are going to make it out of here alive. You are correct, I am not here, and yes Kate, the Kate you must have finally remembered, is dead and never coming back. Those after all were her wishes."

She was being careful and measured with what she said and how she said it. The anger bubbled just under my skin and was ready to pounce at any lie or misrepresentation of my Kate she might try to say. So far she knew exactly what to say.

"After Kate, your Kate, passed you changed, Vincent, and rightfully so. For lack of better terms, you became cold and closed to the world. You helped the Board grow larger than they had dreamed of but you took a life of simplicity and austerity. You were rich beyond most people's dreams but never rejoiced in what you had built or gained. You moved out of your house but refused to sell it. You left it a still monument collecting dust and harboring too many memories. You moved into a studio apartment where you never got to spend much time since you were always at work. You dove into the work and sought refuge from your pain, focusing on the Board and the reincarbonation project."

"The studio apartment you moved into had no luxuries and very little for that matter. An air mattress was your only form of furniture, and your walls and floors were otherwise empty except for a picture of him. In your grief, you adopted a very minimalistic existence while at the same time changing the world."

We both jumped where we sat as the noise of something heavy and determined pounded onto the door. Kate stood, extended her hand to me and the urgency in her eyes was clear as day. We had to move or whatever was on the other side of that door would end us in a matter of seconds. She had one arm and all we had for weapons was a machete neither of us knew how to use. Even in the dire urgency of our current situation, I refused to move.

"You haven't answered me, what are you? After what I just remembered, I really don't care if I become food for the re-soldiers or if I make it out of here."

Kate set her arm down, took a deep breath and nodded. She knew I would not yield on this. "Okay, ba... Vincent. I am not Kate, but I am her. I was programmed from the memories you retained of your Kate. I assure you I am here to help you and have no ulterior motives in accompanying you. I exist for you and keep your life energy safe in case of the worst."

"What?! My life energy? How?"

"What to do with a man who has no interest in anything material? What do you do with a man which wants and needs nothing but what he has lost? Vincent, I am your totem. A walking, talking, caring and loving totem of the only thing you wished you had."

She extended her hand down to me once more. "Please, we need to go." Part of me wanted her to be my Kate. The other part of me wished I remembered what she was talking about and wondered if I should have just walked out into the sea that night.

I took her hand and stood. I went over and grabbed the machete which sat on the coffee table. The pounding on the door continued now accompanied with light creaking sounds of the door starting to lose its integrity.

"We have but one option, Kate." I hated calling her that, she might be named as my Kate, but she was not her, I guess there is more than one Kate in the world. Yea, I can work with that. "Door number one is under siege from a small army of re-soldiers or just one re-soldier on steroids. Door number two sits quietly and classy, but we do not know what awaits us behind it."

Kate gave me that oh too perfect smile since we both knew that it had to be door number two. We approached the door with great urgency. The poor door we had come in through sounded like it was about to stop fighting the mob and give us up. I opened the door with Demetrius's machete at the ready to strike anything that might come out lunging at us. Thankfully nothing came rushing out of the door to try to get us. If I had tried to strike it as it startled us, from the surprise I would have probably missed it completely and cut my own leg instead.

I was right, we had been in an office for administrative assistance with a fancy waiting room in it. The large door opened into a magnificently decorated office. Everything in the office was ultra-modern with sharp lines clean and free of all clutter. The furniture, the table, the bookshelves, and the desk, hell everything in the office was made out of stainless steel, concrete or glass. We walked into the extremely large office, closed and locked the door behind us. The banging on the other door was all but the faintest noise now.

The office had to be a good forty yards long by thirty wide. We started out into the office toward the one thing that had caught our attention above all, the windows by the desk. We might have found our way out of this place and hopefully safety. If we made it, I was obviously going to need to see a shrink, and Kate, well Kate might need to see a mechanic.

We went deeper into the room walking by couches that were large enough to sleep in, amongst other things. They were black leather, very classy but no frill or thrills to them. To the left, opposite of the couch were built-in bookshelves, they were filled with what looked like to be hundreds and hundreds of books but even more interesting than the eclectic selection of books on the shelves was the fact that the bookshelves were made out of concrete so smooth it almost looked like stone.

We kept venturing further into the room, fighting the overwhelming urge to run to the windows, open them and run out of this place. Instead we remained cautious in our approach, we had kept avoiding the "boo" moment from the horror movie I felt we were in and it was just a matter of time in my mind.

The more I looked, the more I noticed the walls were bare.

120

There were no pictures or personal items in the gigantic office. The only thing I could see that might show any kind of personal touch to this office was a single wooden picture frame standing on the glass top of the desk. Whoever was in the picture I could not see, but curiosity was killing me to know who was in it. There were no more doors and really nothing to worry about for the moment, so I made a bee line for the picture frame.

"Welcome. How do you like the place?" Son of a bitch! I jumped and turned, in the room with us now was a man wearing a fancy blue suit and a cheap smile. The bastard had walked out of a bookshelf, yes a bookshelf had swung out like a door, and he had managed to catch and startle us after all.

Kate rushed next to me to seek refuge. I don't know how much help I was going to be, I did have Demetrius's machete, but my skills extended at hacking at the guy with the blade and hoping I didn't drop it. We stood there, huddled together in the ultra-modern office waiting for what the man in the blue suit wanted or was going to do with us. I kept watching the bookshelf door opening, waiting for re-soldiers to start spilling out to destroy us.

"Welcome back. So how do you like it?" The man in the blue suit asked again. The cheap smile hadn't left his face and his dead light blue eyes kept looking at me as if he knew me.

"I see you brought your Kate with you, how romantic. You do remember how to talk or did they disable that when they reincarbonated you, Vincent?"

"How do you know my name?!" I demanded, but part of me knew the answer and the other part of me didn't want to accept it. The man chuckled and for the first time, I swear he blinked, he had been staring at me the whole time without a single blink.

"Oh Vincent, Vincent, Vincent, what happened to you my friend? Don't you remember this place? You don't remember me yet? It will come back, it always does. In the meantime, I must say your new friends have made quite a mess. It is going to take days to replace all the re-soldiers they have taken out. But we have you here now, and it is time for you to come home."

I could feel the anger swelling inside of me. My face got warm and my jaw clamped down grinding my teeth. "Your men took out a great man, and for all I know, they have taken the rest of my team as well. Whoever or whatever you are, I have no interest in telling you what happened to me or answering any of your questions. But you better answer me and answer me quick before I cover this machete with your blood." I spoke slowly enunciating every single syllable so I made sure he completely understood my question. "How do you know my name?"

My grip tightened on the machete and I raised it into an attack position. Well I think it was an attack position, I know I could at least cut some branches if they were on my way; maybe the same technique would work on a man. As I lifted the machete for the first time, I noticed the faint mirage glimmer around it. I turned my head to look at it and the glimmer disappeared but as soon as I took my eye of it and just looked at the blade through my peripheral vision I could see the glimmer. HA! He wasn't giving me a weapon; he was giving me his totem. That sneaky, sneaky D, I had both his totem and his blood.

A quick smile snuck out of my face, I quickly made it disappear and gave the man in the blue suit my meanest most intimidating look while holding the machete. His shit eating grin disappeared from his face. He took a moment, looked down and when he looked back up, all I could see in his eyes was an irritated and annoyed look. He crossed his arms and his well-tailored expensive suit moved gracefully with him.

"You know very well who I am. You just need to allow yourself to remember. Stop trying to figure things according to what you have seen or have been told and just remember. I am getting tired of having to do this every time they come, while they damage and try to destroy what we have built. Just remember, father, look at the picture and remember."

I found myself holding the picture frame without realizing I had grabbed it. Inside the dark wood frame and behind the glass was a picture that I not only recognized but had seen. I looked at it in complete disbelief and memories started to come back, first ever so slowly, then they hit me like waves and my mind went under, as the frame slipped out of my hand and crashed onto the floor. The frame lay on the ground, the glass on it shattered but the picture still intact and haunting. It was the same picture I had seen in the hallway. It was me holding the first patient of the reincarbonation. The young boy who hugged me with all his might but he wasn't just a boy or a patient, he was my son.

# They Grow Up So Fast

The sea of memories pulled me under and I went with it. His grandmother had brought him into my life. His mom had never told me about him after our collegiate transgression and had died during childbirth. He was four by the time I met him. When I found out he was terminal, I could not lose him as the years I had lost with him. I had saved my boy and started a new age of the human species, but the boy was never the same.

I had my boy, but something inside of him changed. It was the first time we ever performed it, and unfortunately there were side effects. They say near death experiences change you, a lot of people see life with a renewed joy and fervor enjoying each day of borrowed time they have. My boy Marcus came back with that furor after the procedure, but it was complete and absolute. Something wasn't captured, we lost something and all that came back was that cold unrelenting drive.

He graduated as young as I had and was always suggesting ways on how to improve the reincarbonation in his years in college. He made sure that when it was time to ask him to join the reincarbonation project, there was no doubt he would accept.

Kate loved him as if he was her own. We never got around to having children of our own, and the big house never got its proper use. He would visit during breaks, but like his father, spent most of the time at the laboratories learning and contributing his new ideas.

With his help, my ideas and concepts took an even larger leap for mankind. He refined the life energy collection procedure and spearheaded the genetic splicing projects. Because of his strong leadership and unrelenting drive, I was able to walk away from the Board to care for Kate and grieve for her once she passed.

Once I came back, the man who had been once my child was almost unrecognizable. His cold unrelenting drive had helped the

Board grow and stretch its reach globally so I just focused on the philanthropic aspect. I should have known better.

After a few years, we were the Board, everyone else had moved and was enjoying the golden parachute retirement money. That is when she entered my life. Oh how I remember meeting her. We were on a trip to Europe and were meeting with several countries courting us for our re-soldier services. We were at a nice cocktail party prior to our dinner when I saw her. She didn't have the muscles nor the braids then, but was even more stunning. We shared good conversation and even greater flirtation over drinks. Tired of being alone, I decided to take her to the dinner with me. The restaurant happily obliged and her speaking several languages was actually quite advantageous in our dinner with the international suitors.

Helena was striking, beautiful, smart and strong, she filled a small part of the big hole I had where my heart once resided. Marcus protested, but seeing me happy for the first time in decades, he relented in his objection to the beautiful German woman. The relationship was passionate and intense. She would travel with me for business, and she would figure out how to turn it into pleasure every time. I once again felt alive and it was wonderful.

I remembered this office. It was mine; I was standing in what once was my office. Why hadn't I noticed before. Disjointed memory after memory kept rushing through me. One of me dying caught my attention, and I went swimming after it.

I saw myself holding my bleeding stomach asking why. My white dress shirt had an ever-growing patch of bright red under my hands as I held my stomach. The pain was excruciating and I could start feeling light headed from the loss of blood. Arms grabbed me from each side and swept me away.

I was on a trip to the Southwest of the United States to meet with different philanthropic groups who were asking for aid for terminal children in Central America. Marcus had stayed back to handle some pressing research or so he said. He was running the Board now and I was a quiet observer and enabler. I could see my one and only son going down a very dark path, lead by his unrelenting drive, but I could not bring myself to do anything about it. Instead I buried myself in what once was the initial mission of the Board.

Helena, as always, had joined me on the trip. I hosted all the organizations at the finest hotels and restaurants I could find. These people did a lot of good work in some very poor and sad places, they deserved me putting on the best I could for them. Helena actually planned it all; she was quite interested and involved in the philanthropic aspect of the reincarbonation project.

After the festivities had finished, Helena had once more planned a night I would not forget. I had learned to trust the frisky German beauty, she never failed to deliver. As we entered our suite, she lowered the straps of her purple dress and gravity won the battle between itself and the friction of her heavenly body. The dress fell and she strutted away from me, nakedly swaying her hips to emphasize her womanly gifts. She told me to go to the bedroom and wait for her. Eager to see what else she had in store for the night; I did as she has so sweetly requested.

I removed my suit, shoes and tie, plopped down on the bed tired from the long day of heart breaking meetings. I cleared my mind, knowing we would help a lot of needy kids after tonight's meeting. It was time to reward myself and Helena was going to be my reward.

"Hello, Mister Rivera" She loved calling me that, she had even learned how to properly roll her r's in my name, rolling them enough but not overemphasizing them. I smiled, lying on the bed and sat up to see what my German lover had in store for me tonight. To my surprise it wasn't a sexy outfit or a nurse's costume. There, naked as the day she was born, stood Helena but

126

with one accessory in her arms. She held a shotgun in her sensuous but solid arms and nowhere to be found was the playful look she always had when she made her grand entrance into the bedroom.

Instead, a serious and intense look filled her face with the beginning of a tear starting to form in her right eye. For a moment, I thought it was a joke, but her expression reassured me I was indeed in a very serious situation and all I was wearing was my white dress shirt and my boxer briefs.

I stood up from the bed, "Please do not move, Vincent" She said as the tear slowly started to roll down her cheek. "I am sorry, but we have to do this. Please Vincent, come with us, we need to stop what Marcus is doing, it has just gone too far."

"What are you talking about, Helena? Who is we? Please put the gun down, babe. I don't know what I did wrong but I can fix it."

Anger rushed into her face, her brow furrowed and her eyes shot daggers through me. "You do need to fix it, and you will Vincent. I see the good work you do, but it doesn't outweigh the harm and deaths caused by the re-soldiers you peddle out into the world."

I stood there in my underwear, dress shirt and now my mouth open. Surprised didn't start to explain how I felt, and the beautiful naked woman holding the gun now looked determined instead of conflicted. "We had tried in so many ways to stop you, Vincent. We have tried talking with the Board directly, but not one of our petitions or suggestions were ever answered much less adopted. We reached out to the media, but any time any brave reporter ran a story about the evil you've been putting out on the world, an even bigger story about the latest sick kid the Board saved overshadowed the truth. While the reporter seemed to find himself or herself without a job and blacklisted. We even tried trying to strike at you laboratory factories and lost a lot of good men and women in the process. This is all we had left, the only thing left for us, and for whatever is worth, I am sorry and I do care about you. We will fix this and you will help us."

I reached my arm out towards her and took a step forward; that is when the shotgun went off. My stomach first felt warmth, and then the pain erupted, bringing me to my knees. I looked down at the origin of my intense pain and under the small little burned holes in my shirt, crimson started to spread. On my knees, I held my stomach, things hurt inside of me I didn't know could hurt. Organs and spaces within me twisted in pain. I looked back up to where Helena stood; her back was now turned to me as she walked out of the suite's bedroom. Two men walked in, one black and muscular the other white, wearing military camouflage and carried me away without me being able to stop them.

# We Do What We Must

I was still looking down at the broken picture and I finally knew. I never left the Board, I was taken. I had been made a fool as they took advantage of my emptiness and sorrow. I didn't know how many times they had brought me back to "help" them, but I had never agreed to reincarbonate nor had I wanted to destroy the Board. There was no Board, just me and my son. I reached for my stomach still feeling the phantom pain of the shotgun blast to it. She had cared about me, but her mission, their mission was more important.

I looked at the one arm Kate next to me, and she saw it in my eyes.

"They are trying to save the people, the people that die every day in the arms of the re-soldiers the Board controls. You don't understand what he has done. While you jetted throughout the world trying to save more lives as you once saved his, he has gone mad with power. Innocent people die and are murdered daily if any defiance is exhibited towards the orders of the Board. Please, baby, help us."

Tears ran down her face and I was fascinated since I didn't realize robots, androids, or whatever she was, could cry. I looked back at Marcus, my boy, I still saw the little kid who would crawl into bed with me during stormy nights. I saw the kid that had so gracefully accepted death until I was able to perfect the reincarbonation process. I remember the numerous incredibly grown up conversations I had with him while we waited for the red tape to clear. Oh I remember how he loved funny movies, the sillier the better, and he loved his popcorn with them. I remember the countless sleepless nights changing damp cloths on his forehead and consoling him from his pain. I saw that boy in the man who stood before me, but I also saw the boy that came back. The arrogance, the entitlement and the sense of holiness he felt for being the first.

I remembered the day he disappeared. He had gone out to play outside in the morning, and it was now dinnertime. He had a tendency to disappear, but food and hunger was always sure to bring him back home before soon. We have had some rough days so I knew he needed his space. I kept trying to deflate what I though was an ego, but that horrific day I discovered it was something much more sinister.

The sun was starting to head down over the horizon and neither my screams nor his stomach was bringing my son back to me. We had a large estate so I decided to search for him in what were his most favorite spots. I searched the pool area, and after not finding him, headed out to his tree house in the middle of the woods. In an effort to make him his own space and help him with the transition, I've had an expert build him in essence a small house suspended up in the trees.

I knew he loved to go there, especially when he wanted to get away from me. The walk through the woods was quite relaxing, even as I was a little panic over his whereabouts. I could finally see his tree house in the distance. His refuge hung from the trees about twenty feet off the ground. There was a wooden spiral staircase that allowed entry to the sanctuary. There also a fireman's pole for quick exit. I kept my eyes on the pole, expecting him to flee away from me once I started to make my way up the stairs.

I climbed the staircase, and even after seeing it many times was taken aback by the beauty and splendor of the tree house. It wasn't large, but it was larger than some of the apartments I lived in while in college. It was made out of timbers, so it perfectly blended into the canopy of the trees. It was round and cedar shingles gave it a supernatural look. It felt as if fairies or hobbits should have lived in it. I made it all the way to the top, and no one had tried to make a quick escape through the fireman's pole. I crossed the rope bridge that connected the staircase and the tree house. It always made me anxious, I knew it could hold twenty men and was perfectly safe, but I always felt as if gravity would fail once I was in the middle, I would get overturned on the bridge and fall down to my death. I pushed past the self-imposed anxiety and reached the deck which was starting to get covered with the orange and red leaves of the fast approaching fall.

I turned the handle on the door and entered a realm that not even my nightmares could have had imagined. The once playful tree house had become a scene of carnage and death. There were rabbits, raccoons, squirrels and other almost unrecognizable animals hanging from the wooden ceiling. They were impaled into metal hooks, some opened up and gutted, their furs covered in blood, others skinned, their naked over exaggerated eyes screaming for mercy. As I moved in between the suspended tortured carcasses, my shoes made sticky and ripping sounds. I looked down just to see the timbers had been stained in blood and piles of guts spread out through it.

The lamp on the desk was on as well as the computer. I focused on the clean electrical devices and ignored the carnage around me for a second as I walked toward them. I moved the mouse and was only more horrified at what I saw. Hybrids of animals and human as animals, Reincarbonation 2.0 he had called it. Even more disgusted by the screen, my eyes once more moved at the hanging death around me. That is when I first noticed and realized why I hadn't been able to recognize all the animals hanging from the hook, some of them where no longer anything nature had created.

My boy, my miracle and once sweet child, was now a twisted boy sewing together parts of different animals together. They were grotesque fleshy colored and still looked moist. They glistened as they hung from the hook heads, bodies and claws fused together to make some sorts of super predators.

The door swung open and my boy stood there carrying a couple more dead subjects for his sick experiments. Ours eyes met, and he dropped the dead rabbit and possum he had in his bloodied hands. Not knowing what else to do, I rushed the young man and struck him in the face with my open palm. He fell down and looked up at me in shock and anger. I grabbed him by the arm and drug him back to the house. I cleaned him up, took him to the car and started driving. I didn't know where I was going, but he needed help and I needed to get him to it.

I started to make calls and finally found our way to the small, private and discrete "rehab" center. It was the loony bin for the rich. I had the means now so I was going to get him the best help money could buy. The young man spent the next five years in therapy and medicated. I thought he was "fixed," obviously I was incredibly mistaken. In front of me I saw the same eyes that I had seen that frightful evening in the woods, but in a man instead of in a boy.

"So you remember, father." He said it as a statement able to read on my face that I knew the truth. "They stole you from me and keep using you time and time again to try to destroy what we built. Please, this is our chance. Come with me, let's set things right, take your seat at the head of the table and rule the Board as you should. I have missed you, father."

As he spoke I saw everything that worried and eventually had scared me about him, but when he said he missed me, oh I saw that young boy who held onto me with a love, trust and devotion unlike any I ever felt. I lowered the machete; I could never use it on him. This was the boy I had advanced medicine and science centuries for; the boy for whom I bent space and time itself. I could never hurt him, even if what the Resistance believed was true. Even if he had become the monster my memories showed me he had become. I could fix him, I saved him from death, saving from madness will be but a walk in the park.

I dropped the shimmering machete and started to walk toward

132

him and his secret bookshelf door. Kate kept begging me to stay, to reconsider, but I belonged with him. My Kate was gone and Helena had been all but a lie. I went around Kate.

"I am sorry but I must go. I am so sorry, but he is my son." She turned after me and kissed me and it felt wonderful and it tasted and smelled of my Kate. I was almost fooled, but only for a second I knew it wasn't her and she would never be, no matter how badly I wanted my Kate back.

I gently moved her aside and continued toward Marcus, I owed him, I made him into this and I needed to figure out how to fix him again. I was half way between the desk where I had left Kate and where Marcus stood awaiting me, so we could make our escape when the giant door we had come through exploded into pieces. Both Marcus and I jumped and ducked at once at the surprise explosion, trying to escape any wooden stakes which might be flung trying to impale us. I found myself on my knees, bent over, and hands over my head protecting myself. I looked up just to see the muscled Helena storm through the door, her braids jumping in the air as she ran in. She seemed injured and was almost covered in blood, whether it was hers or someone else's, I could not tell. Fox covered her back swinging his axe, decapitating the last re-soldier that seemed to be after them.

Behind them a pile of headless bodies lined the floor and the once wooden floor was now a dark red. She walked through the door, and for the first time I saw her for what she really was. I still saw the pain in her eyes for what she had to do, but her conviction was even stronger, making her fight through any indecision.

She walked in holding her machine gun at the ready and my eyes instantly went to Marcus. I now knew there was no master code, no shutdown code to disable the re-soldiers. It was never built into the system. They had used me to get to him, to kill him, to kill my son. They had reincarbonated me, fed me the information as it was advantageous for them to manipulate me, just so I could help them find my son, so they could kill him. The Resistance wanted to end Marcus's reign of terror on the planet, and I had served them my only son on platter for assassination.

I looked over to where he had once been, and all there was left was the concrete bookcase closing him into safety and securing his escape. Shots fired from Helena's machine gun trying to sneak a bullet in through the small gap and hopefully mortally wounding him. I knew my boy, and he was lone gone by now and halfway to safety.

The firing stopped and I was left in what once was my office accompanied by the woman who murdered me for her cause, one of the men who helped her move my dying body and the android they built to keep my life energy. I kind of wished I had snuck out the secret door with Marcus right at this moment.

"We almost had him! Fick dich Miststück!!! Du Hurensohn!!!" Helena screamed and cursed at the bookshelf through where Marcus had escaped. She kicked and overturned every chair, table and even the couch that were close to her. After the muscled woman was done venting her frustration, she turned her attention back to me and Kate.

"How much does he know?" She asked directing the question at Kate, but I replied.

"Everything, Helena, I remember everything." She sighed in disappointment at my response, averting her eyes from mine, instead directing them instead to the floor in front of her.

"Why are you doing this, Helena? Why is the Resistance doing this? Give me a chance, I can fix him, I can help him. I did it once, I know I can do it again. This campaign you are waging on the Board will bring nothing but more deaths. I thought that is what you wanted to end, but instead of stopping death, you are creating it."

Still refusing to meet my eyes, she spoke and brought the last little bit of clarity I was missing. "My name is Ingrid Helena Schwarz, I was the daughter of the Chancellor of Germany when the takeover took place. The Board, your son, activated the override command on the re-soldiers and exterminated most military personnel in most of the countries of the world. Countries panicked as expected and reached out diplomatically to the Board. A meeting was arranged in London which was to be televised and was attended by most every head of stated throughout the world. My father was one of the heads of state leading the conversation with the Board which only sent Marcus."

She said Marcus as if were a curse word with a repulsive look on her face. I was surprised she didn't spit on the ground after saying his name. Her voice was haunting, empty, but full of pain. She continued and since I really didn't have any other options right this minute, I stood there and listened.

"Negotiations went on for days. On the 5$^{th}$ day of the negotiation, it seemed like some compromise to allow countries to maintain their sovereignty was going to be reached. A press conference was scheduled for the next day. Every media outlet was present and ready to televise the future faith of the globe as we knew it. Families of all dignitaries and heads of state attended as well as a show of good faith and trust in the Board, so I was there. Marcus took the podium to the surprise of everyone, the Prime Ministers of the United Kingdom was supposed to have the opening address for the proceeding."

"Marcus got on the podium and started to rave like a mad man. He expressed his indignation toward the politicians and demanded they thank him for ridding the world of war and conflict. He went on and on about how by sacrificing a few soldiers, millions and billions of lives had been saved, saved by him. Even after all the dialogue that had happened those five days, he still believed he did the world a favor instead of a disservice."

"Marcus went on to explain that even though the armies were

disbanded and only under his control now, it was the politicians who really waged the war and prolonged conflict just to ensure their longevity in the system. He claimed the only way to really start over with a peaceful world was to get rid it of all politicians and to make enough of an example so that no one else would want those positions again."

She stopped for a moment to collect herself, and having an idea of where this was going, I remained quiet and allowed her to have her moment. "That is when the re-soldiers paraded all the heads of state and lined them up on their knees for everyone to see. There was a re-soldier behind each and one of them, including my father. They made a line shoulder to shoulder, each with a gun pointed at the back of their heads. Marcus continued ranting and raving about how we should be thanking him, and obviously he hadn't gone far enough the first time, but this time he would make sure the message was loud and peace would be certain."

"Another group of re-soldiers came out from behind this podium, but this time they half encircled all the dignitaries' families. Marcus gave the order and all at once the guns went off behind the dignitaries. I saw my father's first jerk forward then his motionless body slump on the ground as blood rapidly started to surround him. Marcus rant kept getting more agitated after the massacre and the order was given to execute the families. This time the gunshots came randomly and not from where I was expecting them to come from. A few dozen British Special Forces soldiers stormed the proceedings and a firefight broke out. Many of the first families were gunned down either by the re-soldiers executing them or by the fire fight. As far as I know, only one family member survived the massacre along with the British Special Forces soldier who rescued her." She looked at Fox as he still was on the ready, guarding the door with his now blood covered axe.

"I am sorry Helena, I... I don't' know what to say, but I am truly sorry. Killing Marcus won't bring your family back and it will not fix this. Please let me go after him, let me fix this. I started this the day I reincarbonated him, but he is still my son, please just let me try to help him and fix this."

I pleaded with the muscled German woman, but her mind was made up and there was nothing I could do to change it. "I was there, Vincent, I saw what he is capable of, while you were off on your latest bleeding heart trip, your son, the Board, took over the world by brute force and mass execution of the world's leaders."

I stood there not knowing what my next move was going to be. There was no convincing Helena and I could not blame her. I wanted to run to Marcus and help him, but part of me feared he might be too far gone. I was feeling a million emotions and each one of them lead me to another path on what I should do to fix things. All of them kept swirling around my head, trying to distract me from what I was really feeling, what I had to accept but still wasn't ready for. I made this, all of it. I paved the way to this hell with my good intentions and with the love of a father. Still, I had paved the road to a very ugly place and wasn't sure if I could fix it for once.

"Since then, our only recourse has been you. You started this, but you are still good, there is still hope in you. We had to get close to you and that is where I came in. We had to get close to you so we could reach Marcus and end this."

I felt beyond foolish and used. With all my intellect, with every grandiose achievement I had accomplished, I had fallen for her in my loneliness and desperation. Conned into betraying what I fought so hard to once save.

"I am sorry." I heard Helena and looked up at her just in time to see the three flashes to emanate from the barrel of her machine gun. As soon as I saw the three flashes, the now familiar burning sensation broke in my belly and as I remembered, it was followed by shooting pain. I fell to my knees with my eyes changing their focus from the tip to the barrel to Helena's eyes. The same tear I had seen stream down her cheek in my memories was rolling down it once more. She lowered her gun, leaving it hanging from her body and started to walk toward me.

I looked down at my stomach and blood was pouring out of it. I placed my hands on the wounds, trying to apply pressure to stop the bleeding. Kate was at my side once more, but instead of holding my hand, she was helping me to my feet by placing my arm over her shoulders. As she removed my hand from my wounds, the intense pain shot through my body and the profuse bleeding restarted.

Helena was now on my other side focused on what she had to do and denying me any eye contact. One tear was all she had for me, one tear then back to the mission at hand. Fox ran into the room and they exchanged words, I could see their mouths moving through my blurry vision but could not make out what they were saying. He ran to where I had dropped Demetrius's machete, then took point in front of me and the two women carried me out of the office. The two women who had meant so much in my life, but one who had betrayed me by death and the other who had betrayed me by killing me; twice now?

As we headed out of the room, the world swam on me and I could feel my socks once more soaked in liquid, only that this time was my own blood. I bled as they carried me, the pain took over then the world went dark.

I woke up in bed, it seemed like I was in a hotel room of some sort and not a very nice one. "Baby?" I looked to my right and a sweet smiling redhead was holding my hand and giving me a comforting and relieved look. Down the bed and next to the door were two imposing figures. One was a black man who seemed to have muscles on top of muscles, next to him and on the right side of the door was a beautiful muscled and big-breasted woman. Her muscles were as impressive if not more impressive than the black

Adonis, given that she was a woman and still managed to look feminine. Her face was flanked by two perfect braids of her brown hair. On the chair by the window was some sort of military man wearing camouflage. His feet were on the table and he appeared to be sleeping.

I tried to sit up, but the sweet redhead convinced me to remain lying. "Take it easy, baby, it's too early to be running around." I could not resist her smile and remained still. I struggled to ask for water and signaled for it instead. She provided a cup for me to quench my incredibly dry throat. Once I could feel I could talk without razor blades slicing my trachea...

"Hi." All the unfamiliar faces turned and looked at me. Their eyes held an urgency I didn't understand and an even more mysterious relief. "Where am I? What is going on?"

The lounging military man cut me off but not talking to me. "I can't smell them yet but they will come soon." He was glaring at the braided woman by the door. "We tried it your way last time, little girl. This time we do it my way." His tone was stern but held an undertone of caring. The braided beauty by the door lowered her head and nodded in agreement.

After listening to them, a question popped in my head, and it screamed at me. It demanded me to ask it. Lights flashed inside my brain and alarms blared. All other questions became irrelevant in that moment. All I could think, hear and even see was the simple but yet very complex question. So I asked my strange companions the question that needed to be asked.

"Who am I?"